THE RIVER ROAD

ALSO BY KAREN OSBORN

Between Earth and Sky

Patchwork

THE

RIVER

ROAD

a novel

Karen Osborn

WILLIAM MORROW

An Imprint of HarperCollins*Publishers*

This is a work of fiction. All the names, characters, and events
in this book are either products of the author's imagination
or are used fictitiously. Any resemblance to any actual
person, living or dead, is unintended.

HarperCollins books may be purchased for educational,
business, or sales promotional use. For information
please write: Special Markets Department,
HarperCollins Publishers Inc., 10 East 53rd Street,
New York, NY 10022.

FIRST EDITION

Designed by Jo Anne Metsch

Printed on acid-free paper

Library of Congress Cataloging-in-Publication Data has been applied for.

ISBN 0-688-15899-4

02   03   04   05   06   WBC/RRD   10   9   8   7   6   5   4   3   2   1

F

For Jane Gelfman
who understands the process

ACKNOWLEDGMENTS

Thanks to Linda Osborn, Roger King, Corinne Demas, Janet Osborn, Kenton Osborn, Shannon Jenkins, Dawn Evans, and Jane Gelfman who read and made suggestions on versions of the manuscript. Also, Ali Wicks for help with police investigations, the librarians at the Hampshire Law Library, Marilyn McArthur for guidance concerning the local landscape, Ed Klekowski for his talk on the Connecticut River, Kaitlynn Jenkins for help with looking at bridges, and Mike Jenkins for computer support. Thanks to Claire Wachtel for her insight and encouragement and her assistant Jennifer Pooley for all her help.

THE RIVER ROAD

PROLOGUE

Kay

T HE FRENCH KING Bridge was built in the 1930s with the steel arch hidden underneath so that as you drive toward it, only the curved road and thin railing are visible, as if a band of pavement had been thrown across the wide gorge. Named after a nearby landmark, it crosses the Connecticut River where it is joined by the Millers River. Standing on the bridge's walkway one hundred and forty feet above the water, you can follow the river's path far up into the mountains of Vermont and New Hampshire. The soft hills that rise on either side of the gorge are thick with trees.

The night I drove across it with David and his brother, Michael, the bridge was lit with streetlamps, so that from a distance it looked as if it had been strung across the water like a bracelet. The top was down on David's old convertible, and I felt the damp air and squeezed my coat together. Then, just as we entered the bridge, David pulled off to the side of the road.

"Why are you stopping?" Michael asked as he slowed.

"I want to get out and walk across it."

We'd walked across it before. People in the area took drives there on summer days or in the fall when the leaves had turned, parking and walking across to see the view. We had done it at night before also, when no one was around, leaning over the rail and shouting things for the echo.

David lifted the door handle. "Wait a minute," I said as the mechanism inside the door turned over. "We might still be tripping."

"We're not that high anymore," David said, leaning across the seat, his dark hair touching my forehead. "Get out with me and walk across."

We climbed onto the walkway, and I ran my hand along the railing, noticing places where the paint had peeled and the iron had rusted through.

"I don't know what we're doing here," Michael said, following behind us. David and I were home from college on spring break, hanging out with Michael, but Michael hadn't wanted to take the acid. Their parents had had a lot of people over that night, and the three of us had decided to leave the house and go for a drive. Then Michael and David had argued the whole time about who should be driving the car.

"The river's swollen in March," David said, leaning on the rail. "Listen. You can hear it under us." His long body bent over the river. He had let his hair grow out recently, and it fell forward like a fan before he straightened, pushing it back behind his ears. Part of the bank near the bridge had washed away. The sound of the water mixed with the wind that whistled between the posts of the railing.

"This is stupid. I want to get back in the car and drive

home," Michael told us. A van sped past, then a car. David
stopped at the middle, where the bridge was highest.

"I just want to stand here for a minute," he said as I came up
beside him. "You can see the whole sky. Everything is huge. It's
like being on a bike going eighty." He leaned over the railing
again. "I could stay here all night. I could walk on air."

Below us, his words echoed, spreading across the water. I slid
my hand under his. The horizontal rail was rounded and a couple of inches wide all the way around and made of steel, painted
black.

"Screw you!" Michael called out. "I'm getting back in the
car."

"Let him go," David told me. Then, as the car door slammed,
he closed his arms around me. He put his mouth over my
mouth, and everything turned inside out. I could taste the salt
along his teeth. I could drink him up. He unzipped my coat,
and his hands moved under the edge of my shirt. I felt them
slide down across my hips.

"We can jump off it together," he said into my ear, like the
jump off the bridge would be the sex, like that would be the
orgasm. "We can swim across the river. We'll make it. We'll
swim to the side."

I could feel how his back was up against the edge of the rail.
Wherever his fingers touched me, it exploded as if we were
already falling. "I'll go first," he said. "I'll be there."

The light was on in the car, and Michael sat hunched over
the dash. He can see us, I thought, and then David was turning
around. I was warm still where his hands had been. I was exploding again and again, like you could have an orgasm that would

never stop because of being high, like you could go crazy because it would never stop.

He lifted his foot onto the rail. His face was still close to mine, and I could see the sharp lines of his cheekbones and jaw, the large, slightly curved nose, and the high forehead. I could feel where his mouth had been and my lips were wet. Then his foot pulled off the pavement until he was on the rail, crouching there, looking out over the river, my hands helping to steady him. It took a long time for him to stand, his body lengthening, my hands still holding him. As he fell, he looked like a drawing, as if his body were cutting a shape out of the dark, his long arms spread at his sides.

"David!"

I was bent over the rail, watching. The dark turned seamless, as if he were air. And then I put my foot up on the rail, but something came into me where I stopped, where I was outside myself and said stop. Stop it.

Michael was screaming, "David! Shit, David, shit!" echoing.

I don't know how I got off the bridge. The headlights were a pure, blinding white. I couldn't see anything but the lights, and they were exploding the dark.

"These damn lights!" I yelled as I got in the car and Michael began to drive. "I can't see him because of these damn lights. Drive it off the bridge."

"Shut up, Kay. Shut the fuck up."

We drove across the bridge, where Michael turned the car around, and then we had to drive back over it again. It seemed to take forever. I could hear the joints in the pavement passing under the tires. We followed the road to Millers Falls and turned down several different streets until we stopped by a phone booth at a convenience store. While Michael got out to call, I sat staring at the dark lot.

"What happened?" I asked when he got back in the car.

"I called my parents. David jumped off the goddamn bridge." He put his head on the steering wheel and slammed his hand into the dash.

I got out of the car, still trying to piece it together. There was a small light over the phone booth, but other than that, the street was dark. I couldn't figure out where the river was. David was swimming toward the shore. I was thinking how he was there now, how I would go to him and put my body with his body, the body of the river, how I would make love to the river. And then I looked at the car where Michael was bent over the dash, and it cut through me like the acid was gone, exploding as if there were this second again where I could keep him back. David had jumped off the bridge.

PART ONE

—

Kay

EVEN NOW, I hear their voices in my head, calling me, cajoling, interrogating, telling the story again and again, as if you could make sense of it.

"Kay, come here. Look at this."

"Follow me, Kay. This way. Follow me."

I grew up next door to David and Michael on the Connecticut River in a valley divided into small farms. The fields beside the water spread to the hills where the woods begin. Whately, Hatfield, Sunderland, Deerfield—as you drive along the river road, the towns appear. Beside the flat fields a range of hills rises like the soft, uneven humps of a beaver.

I knew the river from the time I was little. On a map in my room I traced its blue course through the mountains of Vermont and New Hampshire, into western Massachusetts past the town where I lived. In July the fields that ran beside it were patterned with flowering squash, pumpkin, tobacco, and corn, and the sky filled with the high hum of insects, the corn leaves rich and dark as if you could peel back the skin of the world.

Months later there would be piles of pumpkin and winter squash, the hills streaked with red maple and yellow birch, the river water layered with the colored leaves that folded into the swirls and eddies. Purple pokeberries and dark red sumac in the old pastures, a small grove of apple trees. I remember it all— the hard sweep of snow in the winter, the barn down the road filled with Holsteins, goldenrod and dried thistles, corn stubble in the fall, and the sound of geese. There were wild roses in the pastures up near the trees and grapevines along the fence by the river. The grass was more than knee high. It scratched my legs as I ran through it, all the way to the water.

For thirteen years while I was growing up, I lived next door to David and Michael. As far back as I can remember, we ran through the fields and pastures by our houses, playing along the banks of the river. David was a sergeant, and Michael and I were captives. Or I was a river queen, and David and Michael were the swordsmen fighting a dragon for the smooth stone that fit the palm of my hand.

Both of them had brown hair and the lanky, long-legged build of their father. Michael's eyes were bright green, the color of the woods, and David's were nearly black, like those stones we picked up from the bottom of the river. During the summer we played in the cornfields, running through the rows of stalks, and when the river was shallow, we waded upstream, the cold water washing around our ankles.

"Kay, watch." An arc of water spread high across the air, until we were soaked and mud-covered, tired enough to lie in the sun and rest.

"When I grow up, I'm traveling everywhere," David told us,

staring at the sky. "To other countries like Europe and Asia and Africa."

"Those are continents," Michael commented.

David turned to me. "You next, Kay. Say what you'll do."

I said I wanted to grow plants.

"Like farmers?" Michael asked. "I could do that."

David lay back again. "Say you could have whatever you wanted," he said, speaking to the sky.

Michael quickly answered fishing. No school.

"A plane," David told us. "One that could land anywhere, something that would fly me."

MY FATHER HAD disappeared before I was born. During their last two years of college, he and my mother had lived together in a house with other students; then, the summer after graduating, he decided to drive out to California with one of his friends. My mother got postcards from Colorado and Arizona, where he camped in state parks, and a letter that was postmarked Nevada, all describing the things he had seen and done.

Over the years mutual friends of theirs would tell us something about him—he married at one point, got divorced, he had a job in the music industry, but my mother had stopped looking for him, and he never contacted us.

A year after I was born, my mother accepted a graduate fellowship in New York City, and a few years later she found a teaching position in the art department at a university in western Massachusetts. When we moved to the valley, we found an extended family in Jen, Kevin, David, and Michael. Kevin taught American history at the state university where my mother taught art, and Jen, who volunteered for an animal-rescue group, took care of me after school and in the summers while my mother worked. Usually it was just Michael and David and me playing together, but sometimes we met up with other kids who lived farther down the road. Jen collected kids the same way she took in hurt animals—cats and dogs, foxes, birds of all kinds, and friends of David or Michael whose parents were going through a divorce or some other hard time.

From when we were little, I looked up to David with a kind of awe, partly because I had no father. In the beginning it was David's father, Kevin, who I looked to. I can remember him coming home in the evenings, throwing his books and briefcase down. He would put his arms around Jen, and then he would scoop up David and Michael in turn, hugging them hard or tossing them into the air. If I was still there, he lifted me also, tucking me against him for a moment so that I felt the roughness of his coat against my face or smelled the scent of coffee.

When I went home afterward, I'd carry the smell and the touch of him with me. "What happened at David and Michael's this afternoon? What was Jen doing?" my mother would ask when I was helping her to make dinner. And when I answered her, I would describe everything that had happened, as if I had inhaled their lives, and that could sustain us.

By the time David, Michael, and I were eleven or twelve, Kevin didn't scoop us up anymore. He had questions for David and Michael—"Do you have homework? Is there basketball

practice tonight?" More and more often we became the audi-
ence for his lectures. Sometimes they were on the importance of
history or certain historical events, as if we were the trial run for
his classes, but he also lectured on school in general, on the
importance of ideas, on paper-writing, athletics, government,
and current events. When we were in high school, David read
whatever his father recommended and effortlessly absorbed his
ideas the way he absorbed everything, but I stood off to the side,
watching. By then it was David I looked up to, David who
could be anything he wanted, David who could jump off a log
into the river, who could run for hours through the woods or a
field of corn, and tie a rope to the branch of a tree swinging far
out over the water.

As we grew older, the three of us became closer instead of
drifting apart. The world we made between us in the fields and
trees or by the water did not let loose. At night we would sneak
out of our houses. "Kay! Come on. Jump, Kay!" I'd hear them
call below my window, and we ran as soon as I landed, our feet
not touching as we leaped through the open air. The fields were
pools of darkness with milky-white streams lit by the moon, a
kingdom of brush and grass, the mysterious high corn and small
animals, the dark, feathery trees and the stars.

The farmhouse that Jen and Kevin bought the year before my
mother and I moved into the small ranch next door always
seemed in the midst of a renovation. They added a family room
onto the back, repaired floors and ceilings, and repainted some
of the rooms. When I was in high school, we ate meals together
or sat around on Jen and Kevin's porch in the evenings, drinking
sodas and talking with Kevin's students who stopped by. My

mother began dating Jonathan, a colleague and friend of Kevin's who spent more and more time at our shared dinners. The family we created was a perfect snapshot, and I couldn't see what lay beneath the surface—my mother's aloneness or Kevin's uneasiness with her friendship with Jen, Michael and David's rivalry or my own insecurities.

During high school, David, Michael, and I still went down to the river to swim or to fish, but now we also smoked cigarettes and drank the beer we confiscated from their kitchen. We got our licenses and drove around together, following dirt roads up into the mountains or into town, where we could hang out at the local store or coffee shop. Several times David and I made out behind the brush along the bank, but he had a girlfriend, Kerry, for more than a year, and I went out for a while with Steve, who was in my grade.

I wanted him even then in ways I couldn't describe, not as a boyfriend necessarily, not as someone to go with to parties or the movies. It was a feeling you couldn't put words to. I wanted to be him, to be in him. I wanted to be what he wanted.

"Swim hard, Kay," he would instruct. "Race me."

Michael, on the other hand, was the person I confided everything to. I argued with my mother over things like curfews and the fact that I didn't care about getting homework done for two years, and in the long talks I had with Michael, I confided everything we'd fought over and what I did with Steve in his car. The only thing I never told him about were the times David and I took off most of our clothes in the thick brush by the river and kissed until our mouths were raw.

After graduating from high school, David enrolled in the university where his father and my mother taught. Of the three of us, he was the one who had been serious about school, taking college-level math and science courses his last year of high school. When we were kids, he had spent hours studying maps and inventing games about traveling around the world. While he was in high school, he had read works of philosophy and complicated books on astronomy, which Michael and I found boring. His senior year he read all of Shakespeare.

" 'O, she doth teach the torches to burn bright!' " he would shout across the river.

And Michael and I yelled back things like "Smoke that torch!"

When David went to go live at the university, I was at loose ends. Most of my friends careened toward graduation with the pursuit of dating and partying, but, having blown off schoolwork for two years, I was forced to take extra courses and spend hours in front of SAT manuals if I wanted to get into college. Michael, who was a year behind me in school, was becoming a serious basketball player, and most of his time was spent in his driveway practicing shots. We still studied together and drank beer hidden by the brush near the river, but we grew bored easily, and when we got into a car, it seemed like we forgot where we were headed.

That spring I was admitted to the university mostly on the strength of my SAT scores, and when I entered the next fall, I was overwhelmed by it. I was taking six classes, five of them given in large lecture halls, requiring a kind of studying I had never been held to. There were parties in the rooms of my dorm late at night, with fans left running by the open windows so that you could smell pot as you walked toward the entrance to the building.

David had a group of friends there already, while I had none. He convinced me that I could handle the precalculus class I'd registered for, and he gave me his notes from a course I was taking that he'd been in the previous year. I saw things about him that I hadn't noticed when we were younger—the way his face was slightly off balance, as if the top and bottom halves didn't match, the look of intensity around the high forehead and dark eyes and, under it, the wide, easy smile. He was driven equally to spend hours in the library or to walk most of the night all over campus. We often met at night, walking to the library together or driving off campus. Sometimes we just wandered around campus. Afterward I'd follow him to his room, where we'd lie in bed, talking some more and making love, then falling asleep pressed like a seam.

It was hard to leave him in the morning, impossible not to want to see him the next evening. We made love everywhere— in our rooms, in the car he sometimes kept on campus, beside a stream we drove to and up in among the trees that bordered the campus.

He didn't go to large parties, and he didn't often drink alcohol, but he had tried smoking pot, and on two occasions when he did drink, he had so much beer that he forgot where he lived and ended up wandering campus most of the night. He did things all at once, as if he couldn't stop, a kind of rush that was there also when he couldn't close a book at three in the morning or walk out of a science lab at night when the janitor was locking everything. He would forget to eat, twenty-four hours or more. I'd find him in his room, bent over his keyboard, having finished thirty pages without looking away. When we drove off campus, he went too fast, accelerating on the curves in the road. Once he pulled over, got out, and sat on the railroad tracks to let the vibrations of an oncoming train rip through him.

When I was examined in court, I wasn't able to explain that about him. It didn't fit with anything else. David spent long hours at the library or in his room, studying and writing papers. He buried himself in chemistry, biology, Shakespeare, Kant, Descartes. He was, as one of his teachers testified, an ideal student.

I WORK IN a radiology lab as a technician, taking pictures of the inside of the body. In the evenings, after my shift is over, I sit staring at the gray films and the forms that seem to be floating on them—curves, twisted tubes, ellipses, slender bones, dark pools. I hold them to the light. Sometimes I feel I am entering sacred territory, an inner sanctum.

In one of his versions of the future, David planned to be a surgeon. I can imagine him at the hospital, looking at the films or replaying a computerized scan. He would take on what was difficult, the astrocytomas or the pictures that show something folded over the heart. When we were kids, there was nothing he was afraid of. He would climb too high in a tree or swim across the river when it was up. And at college he wasn't afraid to enroll in the most difficult courses or to push the speed on his friend's motorcycle up over ninety on roads that cut through the country.

Often I'm here until late at night, eating Chinese carryout and drinking coffee. I sign up for extra shifts, making myself available for emergency-room cases. Dark and transparent, smooth-edged, the films turn luminous when clipped to a panel of light. I handle them too often, like tired questions.

Most of us who work here are in our twenties or early thirties, just married or single, dating each other and meeting for coffee. I am the one who takes work too seriously, is solitary, seldom dates or goes out with the others, does not know how to have fun. I can't quit, even when I am supposed to be gone. One of the radiologists tells me I need to go to medical school. I trace the contours and edges of the films as if I'm memorizing some inner map. Here is the right lung, the fourth rib, I tell myself, the first chamber of the heart.

Even if my friend Craig comes back with a bag of carryout or to look for a jacket he pretends he's left, I can't disconnect.

"Those have already been read," he tells me. Or "You have to learn how to make some sort of other life."

He doesn't know what happened seven years ago, how it rides inside me like a dark reflection. It's early in the morning now, but soon the lab will be full of people. When I'm here working or alone in my apartment, I pull it out again, a chimerical string that unravels with my handling. I could decide to keep going, one day to the next, or instead to swallow the pills I've hoarded in my cabinet.

Sometimes I can feel David with me, as if I could pull him out of the shapes on the films. I pick up a folder with pictures we made yesterday of a forty-five-year-old man with a growth in his chest. I set a marker, increase the size of the image two, three times until the form explodes, radiating tentacles.

Somewhere just behind me, it is as if he has laid his hand on my shoulder. A net of light falls, and everything I see, including the film, turns silver.

Yesterday afternoon the radiologist determined that the small mass was entirely under the ribs, just at the base of the left lung, and clearly operable. I take the films down, marking the area to be looked at again. David is still behind me, a column of light. I close my eyes and let the feeling that is him wash through me.

Afterward it will be worse, everything gone dark and silent, but right now I don't care. I imagine his body as a field I am running through, a spill of light. And I lie down in the field. I let myself dissolve in it.

Michael

S HE COULD RUN faster than we could through the fields and the woods, and she was not afraid to dive into the river. Like a sleek cat, something part wild.

Both of us wanted her from the beginning. "She doesn't have a father," David told me one night when the two of us were lying in our beds in the dark.

"She has to," I said, assuming, even though we'd never seen him, that he was there somehow, coming home from work late at night or traveling.

"He ran off. I heard Mom say. Before Kay was born."

That made her almost mythical, as if she'd been born in the fields with the brush and brambles, sprouted from some kind of seed.

"Kay has no father." I used to think it over and over when I was at school or walking somewhere or playing ball. "She has no dad." As if it gave her a kind of power.

———

WHAT I REMEMBER from when we were growing up is tied to the river. It lived in me, slow and gleaming in late summer or a booming, wild tune in the spring, filled with strange things like the crayfish and minnows we lifted in our nets and carried in buckets to the house.

Kay spread them out across the driveway, arranging them in groups, levels of the dead. We built burial grounds in the fields, mausoleums of cardboard and sticks, pyramids made of mud.

"We can make them alive again if we pour them back in," she said one afternoon as we carried them to the river and, leaning over the bank on our stomachs, dropped them into the water.

"Bless you," she whispered as they fell like arrows through the air. "Swim, dive."

"You guys are nuts," David told us when he saw what we were doing. A year and a half older than me, he always knew more. "Like if you took a dead person back to where they lived, put them in their bed or something, they would start talking again."

"A lesson in futility," he said later.

"Tomorrow they could be growing," Kay insisted. "Like seaweed."

"Lily pads," I added. We were in Kay's backyard, where everything was wet and the grass hadn't been mowed in weeks.

"A couple of fish." David blew his cheeks out and made swimming motions with his hands.

"Glug, glug." I ducked under his waving arms and put my foot over his to see if I could trip him.

"Burial services will be held by the river this afternoon." He went down hard on the ground, faster than I had expected, grabbed me around the knees, and pulled me over on top of him. Then Kay was there, our bodies tangled, the three of us rolling in the grass.

At night after supper I would go outside, even if it was a school night and there was homework. I'd pound the basketball on the drive, slamming it against the backboard until it dropped softly through the net. I wanted to live out there in the yard and sleep in a tent or on the ground, because it was her somehow. Because whatever was the outside was her.

One summer we built forts all day and into the night, walking to each other's house with flashlights and following trails through the fields. Kay kept a notebook with drawings of them and maps showing their locations.

"This is 'Wooded Place,' where we can stay out of the afternoon's heat," she wrote after we built the first one of cut brush that leaned against the saplings we'd cut. The next one was "Jewel," and the entrance to it and its main rooms were marked with stones.

Not far from the house we built a lean-to with a blanket stretched over cut saplings and brush piled on top, and by mid-summer we were building a tree fort close to the river with old pieces of wood, a hammer, and nails. David designed the insides of them, rigging pulleys and building small shelves or furniture of twigs, scraps of cloth, and piles of cut grass. One of the forts was elaborately decorated with chains of wildflowers and small paintings. We had a spyglass, notebooks and maps stored in plastic bags, collections of crayfish, the shell of a turtle. We invented long, involved ceremonies, painting our faces and arms, and spoke in our own language.

It was sometime toward the end of summer when we started taking off our clothes. The first time was during a ceremony. David and I pulled off our shirts, and Kay painted our chests and backs. When she took hers off, we painted blue and red circles on her stomach and colored her small nipples a bright orange.

After that it became the custom to take off everything except our underwear before entering a fort. There were wooden boxes placed next to each fort, where we left our things. We painted each other's skin and made up words: "Blownin, skynar."

By the end of the summer I was caught up in the construction of the tree house, spending hours hammering wood to form walls and tying together a ladder of rope. When I ran out of wood one afternoon, I went to search for David and Kay to help me get more. There were three other forts by now, the lean-to close to the house and two brush forts farther away, reachable by trails we'd worked hard to obscure.

Finding the first fort empty, I ran toward the woods where the second fort was hidden behind a stand of pines. I heard David and Kay before I saw them.

"Let me touch you," David said.

They were in a room made of small cut saplings, and through the leaves I could see their dark skin and Kay's hair.

"Let's kiss again." Kay started laughing, and I heard the way their mouths were touching.

"Ouch, my lips." David pushed her then, lightly. Behind the brush their bodies rolled together on the ground.

I took off my clothes and put them in the wooden crate, inches from where they lay with his arm across her stomach and her hair fanned against his skin.

"It's nighttime," David whispered. "We're alone for years."

"Where's Michael?" she asked him.

I saw David's hand move up to cup her shoulder. "He lives in the tree, with all that wood he's hammering."

"A neighbor," Kay suggested, sighing.

"Yes." David laughed. "A warrior."

I let loose a cry then. It was a game at first, as if I were the one attacking. I took a stick and hit the outside of the wall. I kicked the brush until it fell, collapsing inward.

"Shit!" David yelled out. "Kill him!" His hand came through the brush, and he had my arm, wrenching it.

Instantly my shoulder was hot with pain. I pulled away from his hold, but I knew I was crying. I told myself if I had the long piece of wood I had whittled into a spear, I would drive it into him. Kay was swinging a branch at me.

"Who are you?" she yelled, her face painted half red and half black with a blue line down the center, her hands hot pink.

"It's me, Treenez," I told her.

Kay hit my legs with the branch. "He speaks a foreign language!"

David had a spear now, and he was pushing it against my arms and chest as I tried to wrestle it away. "Capture him! Take him prisoner!"

Everything turned red and hot then, the pain in my shoulder

and my hands on the spear. The pounding inside me exploded, and I kicked David as hard as I could, then swung the spear down on Kay's back and up against David's head.

Kay fell toward the ground, and David lay there, not moving, but I lifted the spear again. I could swing it forever, until they were pulp, I told myself, until they were the ground.

"Stop, just stop!" Kay cried. I could see the places where I had hit her on the back and hip welling up, darkening already. "I can't breathe! I can't see anything!"

I let go of the spear then. David was moving, rubbing the side of his head, and everything inside me was mixed up—the rage, the embarrassment, the confusing way the late-afternoon light was coming through the trees.

"It's suppertime," I told them when I couldn't think of anything to say. My arm was numb now, and the pain in my shoulder was throbbing and almost cold. I took my clothes from the box and walked back down the trail, not stopping until I was at the tree fort again, not noticing how hard the ground was under my bare feet, the grass stiff and sharp.

That evening our parents wanted to know what had happened. I would end up with my arm in a sling, and David would have to be seen by a doctor for a possible concussion. Kay, I was told, was covered with bruises.

"He went crazy," David said. "He got hold of this pole and started swinging it at us. Kay and me couldn't get away."

"David started it. He said, 'Kill him.' He yelled it out."

"It was a game." David looked straight at me. "It was supposed to be a game."

That summer marked the division where it became clearer

and clearer that David and Kay were on one side and I was on the other. I stayed away from them for weeks. School started, and the forts went into ruin. Leaves fell, burying them, and by winter the only one left was the tree fort where I'd nailed the wood. Even now I remember that tree, how the branches were spaced and how wide the trunk was, how all winter I climbed it, standing in the fort until I froze, watching the river run.

THAT NIGHT, AFTER David jumped, Kay and I drove back to the bridge with my parents. "What were you doing out there?" my mother kept asking, as if there were an answer that would make sense. My father just sat there driving, gripping the wheel. All kinds of things were running through my head about the acid and the way I'd watched them practically having sex on the rail of the bridge, then how he'd fallen off it.

When we got to the river, the whole place seemed surreal— the three-quarter moon that I hadn't noticed before over the water, our silence as we got out of the car, the way the wind had died down and everything was still. Then, as we walked toward the bridge, I saw the flashing lights of a police car that had pulled over, and I heard the sound of a two-way radio.

My father ran ahead yelling. "He jumped from the north side. Do you have lights?"

"Kevin, it's me, Greg. I've got searchlights, and I just radioed for more help. Take this light down to the bank, and I'll go up on the bridge. I told them to send a boat."

Kay and my mother followed him onto the bank. I could hear my parents arguing about where to point the light. The officer was Greg Townsend, the father of a kid named Shawn who I played basketball with. "Michael," he called. "Come up here and show me where he jumped from."

I followed him, dizzy from the height. "Here," I said when we got to the center.

"Are you sure?" He ran his finger around the railing like he was measuring it.

"Yeah. That's where he was standing."

Shawn's father turned and held the search lamp above the railing. There was a mark across the top of the rail on the black paint next to where he had touched it with his finger. "From his shoe, I'll bet," he said. Then he held the lamp out over the water, where it lit an area. I could see the waves lapping below us.

"There," he said, pointing, but it was just a play of light on the waves. "Shit."

Farther out, the water wrinkled like black silk. I saw things I didn't want to see. His body would be far under by now, the bottom of the river jagged and rocky, silt rising like clouds of dust, layers of clay and embedded stone. Maybe you continued for a while to see even after you weren't breathing. Maybe you saw what you couldn't see before, details that go past so fast that normally you would miss them—a stone sinking to the floor of the river, a turning leaf.

"Are you sure this is exactly where he jumped from?" Shawn's dad turned from the rail to look at me.

"I think so. It was the middle. He was standing at the middle." Then he held the light up over the pavement where we were standing, and in the fine gravel you could see the partial outline of a sneaker.

"This must be it." He passed the light back and forth again like a wand over the river. "Damn. I can't see anything."

A few minutes later another police car pulled over, and the bridge was swarming with cops. "Hey, kid, how much drugs did you guys have?" One of them pulled me off to the side toward the road and searched me.

"Greg, should we take this kid in and get a urine on him?"

"I didn't even take any of it," I said, pulling away.

He jerked me back by the sleeve of my jacket. "No one's asking you," he said.

"I know the kid," Shawn's father told him. "He's okay. Just find the brother." He was leaning over the water with the light, like if he stood that way long enough, it would show something.

"Shit, Greg. You think there's any chance he's alive?"

"Call in and get a couple of scooters."

Just then my dad came storming up from the bank, walking fast on the pavement of the bridge, not even bothering with the walkway. "I thought you were bringing a boat. Get more light on it. David! Damn, Greg. Don't you have some kind of a horn?"

After that, they got a bullhorn from one of the patrol cars and shouted David's name through it until it echoed to the mountains. My dad paced back and forth between the different policemen and the railing. He grabbed the bullhorn and yelled through it. "Where's that boat?" he kept asking Shawn's dad. "Jesus Christ, how long can this take? Get him out of the damn water."

Another patrol car pulled up, and then, from the south side of

the river, a motorboat approached the bridge. People were rushing back and forth. There were headlights from vehicles, and my
dad kept yelling. After a while he made them bring the boat to
the shore so that he could get on it.

Later on, my mom came out on the bridge and stood next to
me. The boat was on the river again, and I was watching the
lights sweep over the water, soft white globes. I was thinking
they could be seen from a long way under.

"Michael," she said, like she had been crying, "I'm driving
you and Kay home."

I backed away from the rail and started down the walkway off
the bridge. "I'm not going!" Kay was saying. "I won't get into
the car. He's in there. He's in the river."

"We can take her in the patrol car," one of the officers suggested, and I wondered if they had searched her.

"No. Just help me get her in my car."

A few minutes later my mom drove David's car onto the
bridge, close to the walkway. It was a 1974 Ford LTD that David
had bought the summer before for a few hundred dollars from
someone's front lawn, a light blue convertible with long, wide
seats, and even though it was chilly that night, David had insisted
earlier on taking the top down. Now I noticed it was up.

"Michael, get in." The door swung open, and I slid onto the
seat. There was the hum of the heater, the clicking of a blinker.
Then an officer opened the back door of the car, and Kay lay on
the seat crumpled, sobbing.

"Let me stay," she moaned. "He's in the water. I know he's in
the river."

My mother didn't say anything as we pulled out onto the

road. Kay was throwing herself against the door, and I heard the sound of my mother locking the door. "I want to go back," she was crying.

There was this pattern I could feel in me of comfort, all the times we had hung out together talking, especially if David had been ignoring her or had said something that hurt her. "It's okay. Don't get freaked." But another part of me wanted to scream at her, *He's gone! Out of the picture!*

"What were the three of you doing?" my mother said suddenly as she stopped hard for a light. "How could you pull something this stupid?"

"I'm not taking the blame," I told her when the light had changed and we were driving again into the dark. "David has all these fucked-up ideas. I wasn't even on the bridge when it happened. I told him how screwed it was to be up there, and I went back to the car."

"He was up there by himself?"

"Kay was with him."

My mother turned onto our road. In the distance I could see the lights from our house. "Kay," she said staring into the rearview mirror, "I thought all three of you were up there. What happened?"

"Drive back," Kay sobbed, clawing at the seat.

When we reached our house, all the lights were on. My mother got out, and Kay and I stayed in the car. For a while I thought about trying to talk to her. I kept seeing the two of them on the bridge by the railing making out, the way he had his hands in her clothes. "You're still tripping," I told her finally. "This whole night has been nuts."

"Get the key," she moaned, hanging on to me. "Drive us back there." Like another night three years earlier when David had gone to a party with someone else and she kept begging me to go over there with her. "Please, Michael. When we get there, I'll stay in the car. You can go in and find him and tell him I have to talk to him."

When I got out of the car, she was still lying on the seat crying, a soft sound like the drone of a motor. "He might still be in the water. He could swim to the side of the river."

Inside, in the kitchen, Kay's mom and Jonathan had made coffee. They were standing by the sink talking to my mother. "How long ago did he jump?" they asked.

"Around one." My mother fingered her watch, and I could see that her hands were shaking. "More than two hours ago."

Jonathan shook his head grimly. "Do they think he would have been able to swim to the shore?" Kay's mother asked.

"I don't know. They said they would bring some dogs to search. They're still looking."

They all looked over at me as I closed the door. "How did he fall off?"

"He was high. They had taken some drugs."

I saw the dark flush spread across my mother's face. "Tell us what happened, Michael."

"I wasn't even on the damn bridge. You should ask Kay. The two of them walked all the way out. I went back to the car."

My mother lowered her voice so that it sounded unnaturally calm and even. "What were you doing there in the first place?"

"Don't blame me for every stupid thing David comes up

with." I went to move a chair out of the way, and it fell over backward against the floor. "They brought home this acid, and David tried to talk me into it. 'It's clean,' he says. 'A low dose.' I didn't even take any of it." I hit my leg into the leg of the chair. "Ask Kay. She took it with him."

"Where is Kay?" Her mother looked at me anxiously as she moved toward the door.

"She's still in the car."

"Sit down and drink some coffee or something," my mother said, spitting the words at me.

Kay's mom went outside. She left the door open, and I could hear her telling Kay to get out of the car. "How high are you?" she was asking. "I want to find out what happened."

I stood by the table as Jonathan put a cup of black coffee next to me. He lifted the chair and set it upright. The whole time my mother stood still in the middle of the kitchen, like she was rooted there. "There's some acid going around campus," Jonathan told her. "There was somebody talking about it. I've heard that they've treated several kids at the health center who were close to psychotic from it."

My mother glanced at me, then back at Jonathan. "Why would David bring home something like that?"

I threw myself down into the chair. "How the hell do I know? I didn't even take any of it."

When Kay came in, she wasn't crying anymore. Her hair had come undone from the clip that she was wearing, and some of it fell in front of her face. I wanted to pin the strands back up. I wanted to run my hands through it.

"Sit down. Drink some coffee," Jonathan told her.

She stood there for a minute. Finally she sat down at the other end of the table. She didn't look at me.

My mother had started pacing now, back and forth in the small space between the table and the counter, sliding her hands up and down her arms, like if she couldn't stand completely still, she had to keep every part of her moving. "Kay, what happened when David fell?" she asked.

"I don't know." Kay had her head down in her hands, and her hair spilled over them.

"Michael said you were out there on the bridge with him."

"Christ, Mom," I told her, shoving the table hard enough that the coffee spilled over from the cups. "Didn't you hear what I told the cops? He climbed up onto the rail, and then he went over."

"You just told me you were in the car." She stood still again, her mouth open.

I picked up the cup in front of me and drank from it. The coffee scorched my throat, but I kept swallowing. "I was watching. I saw all of it," I said, putting it back down.

"Kay." Her mom sat down next to her, hovering. "What happened? Did he stand on the railing?"

"I don't know. He climbed up there." She had her face down still, staring at the coffee on the table in front of her.

"Did he say anything?" my mother was asking her.

"He said he was going to jump. That he could swim to the shore." She looked up then, and I saw her face. There was a bruise starting to form on her cheek, and her pupils were large and dark in her eyes, like there wasn't anyone inside. "I was supposed to go with him."

My mother walked to the counter and picked up her keys. "I'm driving back out there."

Why? I felt like asking her. *He's gone, water under the bridge; he got swallowed by the air.* I slammed myself against the edge of the table.

Jonathan opened the door for her. "I'll go with you," he told her.

"I want to come, too," Kay's mother said as she stood up and stepped toward the door.

"Someone needs to stay here with Michael and Kay." My mother glanced at me again, her face hard. Another time the year before, when they found out we'd been driving around drinking beer, she'd looked at me that way. "Michael, you should know better than to do something like that," she'd said. David had been in the bathroom throwing up.

"Tell that to David. He's the older one."

"You were the one driving," my father had told me.

"Only because he drank so much he couldn't sit up anymore."

"You could be arrested for that. You could have caused an accident. You could have killed someone."

My mother and Jonathan went out to the car. Once they were gone, Kay started sobbing again. She knocked over the cup that was in front of her, and it broke, a pool of coffee spreading across the wood. I watched her mother get a rag and dig the broom out of the closet to try to get up the pieces.

"I'm taking you home," she said after she'd finished. "Michael, you should go lie down."

"I'm not staying here. I have to drive back out there."

"There's nothing else you can do." Her mother dumped the

pieces from the cup into the trash. "There's nothing any of us can do except hope they find him."

No mention of prayer, no chance of divine intervention. "Maybe he'll appear somewhere," I said sarcastically, looking from Kay to her mother. "Maybe he'll come running down the road in the morning and walk into the house. Hocus-pocus."

"You don't even know what you're saying, Michael. Finish the coffee if you want it, and go lie down."

"He was being such a jerk. He stops the car on the railroad tracks like he's God."

"He didn't." Kay was folded over again, lying across the table. Under the thin sweater I could see the muscles in her back when her hands pounded the table. "He wanted to hear it, not like a god. Like he could." Anything she said came out in a hard, wide moan. "You were watching and he got on it . . ."

"Shut up, Kay." My hand hit the table.

"You walked back off the bridge," she moaned. "Why did you go off the bridge?"

"Shut the fuck up!" I reached over and grabbed on to her hair. Maybe I'll pull all of it out, I thought. Maybe I'll slam her face into the table. Then Kay bent over double and started throwing up.

"Michael." Her mother shoved me back. She made Kay get up and go into the bathroom. "I'm calling Nelson Cray. He said he'd come back over if we needed more help. Go lie down on the couch."

Kay's mother stood there for a moment until I'd gotten up, gone into the family room, and thrown myself down. Lying in the dark, I could hear her cleaning the floor and talking on the phone. After she hung up, she got Kay and opened the outside door.

Once they were gone, there were several minutes before Nelson got there while everything was quiet. What I did didn't make sense because I loved her. I lay there in the dark conjuring her body—the curve of her breasts, her tangled hair—and I saw myself pounding her with my fists, pummeling her over and over until she stopped moving, and then I walked away.

Kevin

———

THE MORNING AFTER he jumps, I'm still standing on the bridge, watching them drag the river. The sky is cloud-covered, a slightly lighter shade of gray than the river, and the temperature's dropped so that I'm feeling the morning chill through the jacket I'm wearing. Two boats at either side of the river pull the wide, weighted net. Periodically they lift it from the water, and I can see what it's collected—a litter of tree limbs and rooted trunks, pieces of rusted metal, an automobile tire, and the frame of a bicycle.

"Go home. I'll call you if we find anything," Greg has said. But I can't leave. I keep walking from the north side of the bridge across the road to the south side, peering out across the water, my eyes scanning the bank. He would have been pulled downstream. If he did make it to the shore, he could have stumbled into the trees, cold and disoriented.

It's after nine o'clock when Ellen drives up and parks her car next to my truck near the bridge. Jen is still at home where Jonathan took her, I hope asleep from the help of the tranquil-

izer he said he would give her. I can hear Ellen talking to Kay as
they get out of their car and come toward me on the bridge's
walkway. I notice things that I wouldn't normally notice, that
Kay is slightly taller than her mother and that they both have the
same thick, curly hair, even though Kay's is dark and Ellen's is
light-colored, almost blond.

"Have they found anything?" Ellen asks when they're standing next to me.

"No." I have my hands on the rail. It is just narrow enough
that I can curl my numb fingers over it and touch the underside.
I realize I'm leaning my weight into it.

"What are they doing?" Ellen asks, pointing. I can hear the
pinched sound in her voice, but Kay seems oddly calm, her
expression blank as a sleepwalker's. There's a dark bruise on her
face beneath her right eye.

"They're dragging the bottom," I tell her.

Ellen has been a friend for years now; both she and Kay
spend a lot of time at our house. When we first moved here, Jen
hated living along the river, isolated in an old farmhouse with
two kids all day. I can remember the relief I felt when Ellen
moved into the house next to ours. Jen had been saying for
months by then that she wanted to move somewhere more pop-
ulated, but I had loved the valley from the first time I saw it,
with its river and the farmland and the nearby mountains, all
layered with a history so tangible you felt you could hold it in
your hand.

Shortly after Ellen moved in, the two of them began talking
every evening on the phone, and Jen would often go over and

visit with Ellen when she was in the barn behind her house, which she'd turned into a studio where she made her sculptures. Ellen leads what I have always thought of as the unrestrained life of an artist. She moved here as a single mother. When the kids were little, I almost thought of Kay as my daughter. I remember sitting in an armchair with her and Michael on my lap, reading to them. Now, as I glance at her and look down at the hand Ellen's placed on my arm, it occurs to me there are things I don't know about either of them.

"Is there any way he could still be alive?" Ellen asks as she looks out over the water.

"No," I tell her. "They say there's probably not."

Kay pulls her coat closed. The bruise on her face is the kind you get when someone hits you. I haven't felt comfortable all year with her and David's seeing one another. They were too close as children, and as Kay got older, she became so emotional, almost high-strung. It seemed the whole thing could end up being too intense, a distraction, I told David, from the studying he needed to do at college.

"What happened to your face?" I ask her.

"I don't know." She touches the skin lightly with her finger. There's swelling under the eye and a fine network of blood vessels across the bridge of her nose. The bruise itself spreads like an inkblot.

I glance at Ellen. "It looks like someone hit her."

Ellen turns from the water, a little sharply. She steps back from the rail and puts her hand on Kay's shoulder. "She could have fallen against something last night."

I stare at the water again, confused about why they're here. Then for a few seconds I have the odd sense that none of it's actually happened. "I've been standing here since they brought the boat back, trying to imagine the way he must have fallen, how fast his body went through the air, what it felt like when he hit the water," I tell them, as if that will make it real.

Ellen stands next to me looking down over the rail, watching the boats. I think about asking Kay why they were out on the bridge in the first place last night. I haven't been able to form any kind of context. David hadn't used drugs before. There were a few incidents in high school involving alcohol, but nothing extreme. He was an exceptional student, good at enough subjects that his choice of majors was almost limitless. By contrast, Kay lacked the discipline for studying. Her grades were mediocre. "Whose idea was the acid?" I ask her.

She seems taken aback. "David brought it home with him," she says, her voice so quiet I can barely hear her.

"I should get Kay off the bridge," Ellen tells me, stepping back from the rail.

"How did it happen? What were you guys doing out here?" I ask her, but they've already started to move away with Kay in front, and they keep walking, as if they can't hear me.

They've almost reached the end of the bridge when Kay slumps over, and I see Ellen put an arm around her shoulder. Then Kay straightens up again, and they walk toward their car. When they're gone, I turn back and watch the net that gets dragged up again and emptied. You think you know people, but when something like this happens, you really don't know anyone at all.

THE REST OF the day washes away, until by afternoon I can't tell what's happened. I go home and drink coffee. I shouldn't be functioning anymore, but it's like I'm turned on high speed, able to drive over sixty on back roads or walk for miles, my brain clicking over each detail, the way you do when you've been up late working against a deadline, taking in and categorizing each piece of information, absorbing none of it—the scuff mark, the depth of the water, the number of scooters that were on the river from 2:00 A.M. until dawn, and the number of hours they've dragged the bottom.

When I'm in the house, I see or feel him everywhere I look. In the kitchen he's there digging through the refrigerator, and when I sit on the couch in the family room, I sense him next to me, the dark hair and eyes, the bright energy. By now Jen is awake, moving through the rooms like a shadow. She comes up to me, and for a moment she puts her arms around my shoulders. Then the phone rings, and I hear her talking to one of her friends. "He and Kay walked out to the middle," she tells them. "They were both high on acid."

"Why are you telling people that?" I ask when she gets off.

"Because it's what happened." She walks over to the sink and rinses off a glass that's on the counter. Whenever he drank a glass of milk, he used to tip his head back and swallow it all at once.

I stand there for a moment watching her, seeing David, then not seeing him. Her back and neck curve over the running water. "Do you have to talk to anyone about it right now? We don't even have all the facts yet."

She turns around and leans against the counter. She is still wearing the white turtleneck she had on the night before, and there are smudges and stains across it. A water mark spreads up one of the sleeves. "Greg said they think he and Kay were high from the acid and that he jumped."

I stare at her for a moment. Her eyes are bloodshot, and there are small dark areas under them. Her fingers are picking at the sleeve. "No one really knows that yet," I tell her.

For a moment longer our eyes rest on each other's, and then she looks away, her shoulders narrowing and her chest collapsing like she's starting to cry. "Maybe we won't ever know exactly what happened," she says.

When the police come out and talk to Michael, he sits with them for over an hour in the family room, sullen and quiet. From the kitchen I can hear his mumbled responses. "I don't know," he tells them. "It was dark. I'm not sure."

After they've left, I go into the room and sit down next to him. Across from us is the armchair rocker that David used to sit in whenever he was in the family room listening to music or reading or watching TV. If Michael was in it already and wouldn't surrender it, there would sometimes be a fight.

"You were with David all night," I tell Michael. "You need to say what happened." He is looking out the window, and for a moment I follow his gaze. Through the glass you can see the basketball hoop I helped him set up at the end of the driveway several years ago. Just yesterday afternoon he and David were playing one-on-one, and I sat here watching them.

Michael folds his long legs awkwardly underneath him and buries his face in the cushion he's holding. "You couldn't tell David what to do," he says into the cushion. "He wouldn't come off the bridge."

"Why not?"

He sits there for a few moments, not answering. The sun moves from behind a cloud, and the pavement, wet from the snow that's recently melted, gleams. "What were he and Kay doing while they were standing there?"

I can hear the breath he takes in and the quick exhale. "I don't know."

I try to put my arm around the wall of his shoulders, but he shrugs it off. The sun moves behind the clouds again, and the air darkens. After a while I get up and walk out the door onto the driveway. All it takes is the trick of light or the quick turn of the head and you could think you see him running through the yard or disappearing behind the barn. I am not a person who prays, and so what I say to myself over and over again is a kind of incantation: He is out there still, wandering around, cold and disoriented. Then I get in my truck and drive back down to the river.

HOURS LATER, AFTER I've gone home again Greg calls to say that they're going to have to quit dragging the river. "We've had this problem before in the spring when the water level is up with the ice that's just melted. Things get caught in the debris.

Once the water falls back a little or the current changes, they work their way free and we find them downstream."

"What about sending a diver down there?" I ask him.

"This time of year, when the current's so strong, it's too dangerous. We'll keep patrolling the area and watching the water near the bank in case something washes up." He pauses, and I'm conscious of the receiver's weight in my hand. "Eventually it will."

He will, I want to say, but I'm quiet, trying to wrap my brain around what he's said.

"Did you question Kay Richards yet?" I ask finally.

"Yes," he says. "I took down her statement."

"What did she tell you?"

"There was nothing substantially new as far as the search is concerned."

I hear him shift the receiver, breathing out heavily. "My guess is that he was pretty high, tripping from the LSD. Right now I'm assuming he got up on the rail because his judgment was impaired. Then he fell off or jumped. You know as well as I do that other kids have jumped off that bridge. There were those college boys who got drunk and jumped from that same bridge a few years ago. He could have done it as a prank, or it could have been part of a delusion."

It's quiet for a few seconds, and I can hear the shuffling of papers. "None of this really adds up," I tell him. "His supposedly taking the acid and jumping off the bridge. It doesn't fit with him."

"Sometimes parents are blind to certain aspects of their kids," Greg says slowly.

I take a quick breath in. "I'm not," I tell him.

"All right." Then it's quiet for a minute, and I can picture him fingering his mustache. "I'm really sorry about this. I'll call you if I find anything else."

Later that night Jen and I start arguing. At first it's over small, almost petty things. She wants to know what I've told my father and my sister, and she insists we need to think about having to plan a service.

"Are they coming out here?" she asks as I walk through the kitchen.

I stop in front of the table where she's sitting with a pad of paper in front of her, writing out some kind of list. "I don't know," I tell her.

"Have you told them?" She turns the pen in her hand.

"Of course," I tell her, when actually I've only talked to my father, who has probably told my sister and her family.

She writes something else down on her list. "Are they coming? You need to find out when they're coming here."

"What are you writing?" I ask, peering at the letters. Ever since I've known her, she has written up lists. When we lived in Washington, D.C., and she was working for the animal-rights group, she used to tape them to the refrigerator and sometimes even to the walls of the kitchen.

"Nothing," she says now, starting to cry. "I'm trying to figure out what to do with it all. They said it could be weeks before they find a body, and what if they don't? What are we going to do then? How long will they keep looking for him?"

Forever, I feel like telling her. *I want them to look forever.* "They're still patrolling the shore," I say instead, turning away from the table and looking out the window at the spot where a line of trees divides us from the road. "I want to know what happened. David wouldn't have jumped off that bridge."

"He had taken a drug. You don't know what he would have done. He could have fallen."

"He wouldn't have taken the drugs like that and jumped. There was no precedent."

She gets up and goes to the counter, where she pulls a tissue from the box and blows her nose. "We don't know that. Last summer when he was living here, he was out almost every night. We had no idea—"

"He was nineteen years old last summer," I tell her, turning sharply from the window. "He had two different jobs."

"I can't talk about this," she says.

"Last night, when you came back out to the bridge, you said that Kay had told you that she was supposed to go with him. What did she mean by that?"

Jen blows her nose again, crying audibly. "She was saying all kinds of things. I don't think she knew what she was saying. Why are you asking that?"

"I don't know." I'm picturing Kay at fourteen or fifteen, when she started wearing tight-fitting clothing and was clearly flirting with both of them. I'm remembering how uncomfortable that made me. "David was out with her constantly during Christmas break. He's not normally like that. She had her hands all over him when they were in the house. I wouldn't be surprised if she pursued him on campus. That's probably why his grades weren't as good last fall."

"I don't want to talk about this," Jen says, pushing the chair back under the table as she walks out of the room.

THE NEXT DAY I still haven't really slept, and I'm in high gear again, my brain racing ahead with every phone call we get, processing the information. One of his shoes is found, washed ashore. I call Greg and convince him to search again for several hours with the dogs. Neighbors and friends keep stopping by to ask what happened or how they can help us. Someone sends flowers.

At midday I drive out to the bridge to watch the search they're conducting. There are two German shepherds, specially trained to follow the scent from an article of clothing. When David was younger, we had a pair of retrievers, and he and I used to take them out hunting in the fall for ducks. It would be early in the morning, the world still gray and unformed as we waded through the reeds and marsh, sharing coffee from the thermos. I wanted the experience with him more than getting the bird. Sometimes we would just watch them flying across the water.

We'd talk during those hours. I explained my theories about historical cycles. He shared my appreciation for the local area, with its history literally under our feet—the glacial rocks and fossils from the prehistoric lake, colonial houses that can still be seen as you drive through the valley. Only once do I remember

David's actually shooting a bird, and he was so quiet afterward that I thought he was saddened by it.

The German shepherds sniff at the jacket and T-shirt I've given them. Then the officer gives a command, and they weave uncertainly along the shoreline, noses to the ground. I can picture David like one of the birds, high above us, blood falling from the dark place on his breast.

"The chances of them coming up with anything are slim," Greg says as we stand there watching them.

"There was the shoe."

Greg lifts his hand, signaling one of the officers with the dogs. "He would have tried to get those off first, if he was thinking clearly," he says. "You know that."

I don't say anything. I walk down to the river and put my hand in the water. He has no idea of the image he's conjured—David under the dark water struggling with the shoe, pulled by a sudden current. I'm wondering for how long he was panicked.

"I want you to keep looking," I tell him when I hear his footsteps behind me. "If he made it to the shore, he would have been exhausted and maybe disoriented. Have you checked with all the residents who live nearby?"

"It's been in the newspapers and on television. Most of them have seen us out here." He starts back up the bank. The hand I've had in the water is numb. "Kevin, I'm sorry, but it looks like he wasn't found in time."

That night I don't sleep much again. Around two o'clock I get up and pace the downstairs part of the house, riffling through the notes I've made when talking with the police and watching the late-night news on the chance they could broadcast something I don't already know. Then, in the early hours of morning, I get in my truck and drive out there again. The moon is full over the river, illuminating the water with a gauzy light. I cross the road and look over the south side of the bridge, where the tributary joins the river, widening it. My eyes travel, moving downstream. There are areas nearby that I explored once with David and Michael, cliffs and layers of sedimentary rock with plants growing on the rock shelves. Noises travel from far away—the barking of a dog, the snap of a branch, the rustle of leaves. I focus on the banks, looking for the caves that I know are along them, when suddenly I see a form a quarter of a mile or so downstream, floating near the left bank—a longish shape, gray in the moonlight.

It takes me an hour or more to scramble down the bank, then pick my way along the shore, stumbling over rocks and tree limbs and into deep pools of water. As the sky lightens, I can see more—a grassy marsh in the distance, deer standing near the trees, swallows and osprey. I remember canoe trips we've taken down the river, Jen and I in one and the boys in the other, paddling. Sometimes they would argue, and Jen and I would have to split up, each riding with one of them.

By the time I reach what I think is the area I spotted from the bridge, I am wet and chilled and I can't find what it was I thought I saw from the bridge. There's a log near shore, and I tell myself maybe that was the form, but it's dark and partially submerged. I end up walking farther and don't start back until after daylight.

In the morning I can't get Greg to send anyone else out with the scooters or to patrol the shore. Finally, at nine, he drives out himself and stands with me on the bridge, but I can't find the form I saw so clearly five hours earlier. "You could have seen anything from here," he says. "At night it's impossible to really see—even with searchlights. There are too many shadows."

He convinces me finally to go into the restaurant nearby and order coffee and breakfast. He wants a serious talk about how I'm handling things. The inside of the restaurant looks like a hunting lodge, with deer and moose heads hanging on the wall. The table we're seated at has a green tablecloth on it, set with worn white plates, cups, and saucers. The place is partially full, and the waitresses bustle about, enjoying the activity.

"I imagine all this has been good for business," I comment.

"Don't be like that," he says. "People don't see it that way."

Our eggs arrive, and I sit staring at the plate. "I have a son the same age," Greg reminds me as he cuts into his. "I can imagine what you're going through."

I nod. I've seen the same assumption made by my students, but the matter of perspective warps everything, making it impossible to put yourself into another's shoes. Once you approach the past with that knowledge, you see how isolated each of us is, living our lives in a thin period of space and time. Any connection we make seems miraculous.

He tells me about other tragedies that have happened to kids, how one teenage boy blew his friend's brains out by mistake, and there was that carload of them two years ago that were involved in a horrible accident.

"Let me follow you home," he says at last as he finishes his coffee. "Have you phoned your doctor since this happened?

Exhaustion can become dangerous. I'm sure there's something he could prescribe to make you sleep."

"I don't want to sleep," I tell him, pushing aside the half-finished plate of eggs and hash browns. "I want to take all of it in."

He tells me I can't. He says, "That is just the kind of statement that concerns me."

When I finally agree to check with my doctor, he signals to the waitress for the check. "How is Jen?" he asks as we leave the table.

"She's falling apart," I tell him. "But she's starting to think about planning some kind of a service."

"That's good," he says.

We walk out to the parking lot then, but as I start to climb into the truck, I change my mind. "I'm sticking around for a while," I tell Greg as I close the door to the cab.

"Go home," Greg tells me, standing beside his patrol car. "Let me follow you. You're too exhausted to stay out here."

"I just want to walk down the bank again and get another look."

He shoves his keys back into his pocket and walks over to the truck. "I hate to have to say this to you," he tells me, staring at some point past me, maybe at the trees or at the river itself. "But you have to realize by now, it's unlikely we'll find him alive. The chances go down each hour after something like this happens, and it's been a couple of days now. He was a strong kid, a good swimmer, so you hope against hope that he had the ability to pull against the current, but this time of year with the water so high and still close to freezing, it was unlikely from the beginning."

I glance down at the pavement. A few areas of slush still mark the roadside. "Kevin, you know what I'm talking about," he continues, looking directly at me. His face is deeply lined, painfully, I think to myself, yes, painfully. "Because of the height of that bridge and the depth of the water, the temperature, the current—any one of those things would make it highly unlikely that he would even have survived the fall. Together they make it pretty much impossible."

He's quiet then, and we both turn and look out at the bridge. It curves innocently, high over the water, stretching the width of the deep gorge. From where we stand, you can see the statues of the eagles that mark the entrance of the bridge. "You need to let go," he says quietly.

I shove my hands deep into my pockets. "I am not letting him go," I tell him. "I am not."

We stand there for a few more minutes, staring at the bridge and the long drop into the gorge beneath it. Then I hear the keys in his hand again. "I guess I could send out a couple of men to search the banks," he says.

"What about using the water scooters? They get in close to the shore more easily."

"That's a much larger operation," he says. "I'm not sure that it would really do any good at this point."

I turn and look at him for a minute. He's known both David and Michael since they were kids. His own son, Shawn, sometimes hangs out at our house, and if circumstances had been different, he could have been at our house that night.

"All right. I'll try to send up a scooter." He closes his fist around his keys.

I look back out across the river. "Thank you."

"Take care of yourself." He slaps me on the shoulder.

I stand there for a while longer, listening to him get into his patrol car and start the engine. After he's driven away, I take out the pair of binoculars from the glove compartment of the truck and carry them down to the bridge, where I stand on the south side scanning the bank. Using the binoculars, I bring small areas into focus, meticulously checking each square foot, trying to steady my hands and keep track of my progress. My eyes play tricks on me. A fallen tree seems to have a bit of blue on it. There's the movement of a small animal. Sometimes I lose my orientation and have to start over again. It's the kind of thing I've been trained for—close observation, the consideration of perspective, and the recognition from a distance of significant detail.

Behind me, cars and the occasional truck thunder over the bridge. The sun has risen higher than the clouds along the horizon now, and when I lower the binoculars for a moment, I notice that the buds on the trees along the riverbank are slightly pink, so that if you open your eyes wide to take it all in at once, the shore is rose-colored.

He's gone, part of me is saying. Even if his body doesn't get found. Then I force the binoculars back up against my face and go back to checking each section of the river.

PART TWO

Kay

———

WHAT I REMEMBER of him are pieces, like translucent images. Sometimes I dream he is nearby, walking the streets of the city I live in or calling from a stand of trees. If I follow the sound of his voice, I wake up, and he disappears.

It's past eleven when he comes running across the road from the dorm where he lives. The night is cold, the kind of temperature that will kill any flowers still blooming, and I shiver as I put on the jacket I've brought with me. I can hear his boots on the pavement.

"Kay," he calls out, standing under the lights.

He closes his arms around my shoulders, and the cold that is on him goes through me. I touch the smooth, hard lines of his face, his dark hair. "I've got the keys to Chad's bike," he says, jingling them in his pocket. "I rode it earlier up toward the hill towns."

We run down to the parking lot, not feeling the cold. As he

unlocks the bike and gets on, I take an elastic from my pocket and tie back my hair. "Hold on to me," he says. "Don't let go."

He pulls out then, and I put my arms around him as he drives toward the main road, kicking up the speed. We take a corner, and the bike leans into the curve, hugging it tight, squeezed by the air. I can feel the softness of his flannel shirt inside the denim jacket. The button under my fingers is broken, and the material is frayed. Beneath it, the muscles of his stomach harden like a knot.

In places the darkness is lit with a floodlight from someone's house, a yellow window, a sign, or a passing car. Neither of us has on a helmet, and the wind rips through our hair. He shoves his foot against the throttle, and the bike peels away from the pavement. My ankle brushes the hot metal that covers the tailpipe. When I grip the seat, the vibration from the motor sizzles through me as if I am a circuit. I flatten myself against him, and everything is blurred by the speed—the undefined shapes of barns and houses, headlights, the cab of a truck. I tighten my arms and swallow the air.

By the time we turn back onto the campus, I am nearly electrical. We climb off the bike and run up the dark hill. David's dorm is coed, making any precaution we take seem absurd. The individuals in charge are locked in their rooms, asleep. We make jokes about this. "They are ever vigilant, ever observant," I say.

"Like rocks," he replies. We climb the back stairs calling out words that seem ludicrous—"daffodils," "turtles," "fire."

David's room is a tight cubicle crowded with books and clothes. We fall onto the narrow bed, laughing and whispering.

He says there was a party next door earlier with twenty people or more, everybody high.

We twist around each other, we collide. The soft flannel of his shirt brushes against my neck and face. I open my mouth, and there's no way to tell which tongue is mine. I think of the speed we went at and the dark air. When we take off our clothes, the places where my skin is still cold could be fire.

Afterward he'll walk me back to my room. When he's gone, I'll stand at the window, watching as he makes his way to his building. Later I'll remember the way he looked, the curve of his shoulders and how he disappeared slowly as he moved farther away from me, past the streetlamps, into the darkening air.

THE NIGHT DAVID jumped from the bridge, my mother kept asking me questions. She wanted to know where the acid came from, what had happened to my face, and why we were standing at the edge of the bridge.

"Did you know he was going to jump? Did he say anything? Were you fooling around?"

Later, when I lay down in my bed and closed my eyes, I saw what had happened spinning out in forward and then reverse, stopping at certain frames like frozen animation.

By morning when I woke up, nothing made any sense—the way the doors opened and closed to different rooms or the sunlight that poured through the windows drenching the walls and carpet.

"Eat some cereal," my mother said, handing me a bowl.

Everything I heard filtered through a sound that was in my head, a maddening hum, the way you would hear if you were underwater. My movement was like that also, slow and directionless, a kind of vertigo.

"Kay, hurry and get dressed."

Then I realized it was my own heartbeat I was hearing. *David jumped off the goddamn bridge.*

I couldn't get dressed, couldn't make my body go any way that I needed it to go. Then I started to shiver all over, as if I were saturated with adrenaline, but the feeling of having to sprint was mixed in with the heavy dread of knowing that something horrible had happened that couldn't be reversed, like the cold sweat of a nightmare.

After I had managed to pull on a pair of pants, my mother grabbed a jacket of mine from the hall closet and told me to get in the car. "Here, Kay. Drink this first," she said, handing me a cup of warm coffee as I moved toward the door. It ran out the corners of my mouth when I couldn't swallow.

"Shit. Kay, wake up." She took the cup and tossed it into the sink, wiped at my shirt with a dishcloth.

When we got in the car, I must have been crying, because she was telling me to stop. "This is hard enough. I'm trying to get you out there so we can see if they found him." I couldn't feel anything. The sun was so bright coming through the windshield that I couldn't see anything. *These damn lights. I can't see him because of these damn lights.* It got inside my head. It filled the inside of the car.

When we reached the bridge, it seemed huge now that there was light everywhere. Long spaces stretched out between the joints in the pavement, and the railing was above eye level, so that I couldn't see the river that was under it. David's father stood turned away from the road in the middle by the railing. His truck was pulled off to the side with two police cars.

After we stopped, small things brought it back—the car door opening, my foot on the gravel pavement. *"Wait a minute. We might still be tripping."* Like it was still echoing.

"I'm going to ask what they've found," my mother said as she got out. "You can wait here if you want to."

I followed her as she climbed up onto the bridge. The brightness of the sky made everything panoramic, like a wide-angle Kodak shot. The river was gray and churned up beneath us. It didn't seem like where we had been. The bridge swayed every time a car or a truck went past us. "Shit." I had to stop and hold on to the railing.

"Kay." My mother turned around and walked back to me, a deep crease between her eyes, like her forehead had been squeezed together.

"Go on," I said, pushing her away.

By the time we reached David's father, I was certain it was all wrong. "It was another bridge."

He turned and glanced at me, like he hadn't heard what I'd said. Disconnected words went around inside my head. "Falling." "On air." "Some other bridge."

"Jen went home hours ago," he told my mother. "She was falling apart." He turned away from us again and stared out over the river. Then I saw it in the gravel next to Kevin's shoe, like a piece of glitter, the back I'd lost from the post of my earring.

"What are they doing?" my mother asked.

David's father leaned over the river. I could see the grip he had on the railing. "They're dragging the bottom."

My mother said something else, but I couldn't hear what it was because of the trucks behind us, or maybe it was the sound again of my heart. I touched the railing and saw the black paint and the rust spots peeling. I looked down into the river. Wherever the sun touched the water, there was a place like a dark mirror, thousands of tiny dark mirrors winking. When I was in high school, I had listened once to divers talk about the river and how it was impossible even with lights to see anything underwater in the spring because there was so much silt. It would cover your mask.

My mother and David's father kept talking, and pieces of what they said fell through like there was a sieve in my head. They were dragging the bottom of the river. The weeds would have died back in the winter. There would be rocks, maybe some dark green moss, and the silt, and the decomposing leaves. Closer to shore, fallen tree trunks and branches.

My mother's hand held my elbow, and we were walking off the bridge. Then I leaned over the rail for a second as my mother put her hand on my back.

"He drowned, didn't he?" I said.

She opened the car door, got in, and turned the key in the ignition. "We don't know that yet. We don't know anything for sure."

AFTERWARD WE DROVE to the university. My mother said things about a police investigation and how they would probably search my dorm room. She said she didn't want this to ruin my life.

"Do you have any drugs in your room?" she asked me. I was standing at the window looking across the quad where David's dorm was. The door to my room was open, and the halls were quiet. "Kay," she said, "you need to be honest with me."

"No. I haven't even taken anything like that before. I tried smoking pot, but just once in David's room when a friend of his brought some in." She kept opening the drawers of my desk and dresser, like she wasn't listening to me. She pulled the blankets off my bed and shook them out, then got down on her hands and knees searching under it.

"Would your roommate have anything?" she asked as she dug through the pockets of a pair of jeans she had pulled out from under the bed.

I thought about Sara. We had sometimes helped each other with a psychology course we were both taking. Twice we had gone to see a movie together on campus. She knew I was seeing David. "I don't think so," I said.

My mother got up off the floor without even looking at me.

She went over to Sara's dresser and pulled the drawers out, running her hands through the clothes that were in them. By the time we left, she had found a small bottle of vodka, which she threw into a Dumpster before we left the campus.

I think we drove home after that. Later I know the police came to our house. I had been sitting on the floor in the kitchen listening to my mother on the phone, first with Jonathan trying to find out what was going on, then with a friend of hers asking if she thought that we should look for a lawyer.

"Kay says she doesn't know anything about where he got it, and there weren't any drugs found on her. She said that David brought it with him from school."

Then the police rang the doorbell, and she said, "I have to get off the phone."

There were two officers, Mr. Townsend, an older, heavyset man with thick, graying hair and a mustache, who I recognized as the father of one of the guys Michael played basketball with, and Mr. Sadoski, a younger officer who had once come to our school as part of an antidrug program. They had on uniforms and presented their badges. I heard Officer Townsend apologize to my mother for the intrusion.

My mother led them into the kitchen. Someone turned on a light, and I remember how bright it seemed, how it washed over the rest of the room, bleaching it. Then Officer Townsend sat down across from me at the table and asked if it was okay if he called me Kay. The other officer stood by the counter with a spiral pad for taking notes. They had a few questions, they said, about what had happened the night before. They needed to get my statement.

At first what Officer Townsend asked me was directed at the drugs. He wanted to know where they had come from. I told him that David had brought them home with him from the university.

"Where did he get them from at the university?"

I told him I didn't know.

"Did David do any drugs in the past that you knew of?" he asked. "Do you remember ever knowing that he had taken or possessed any drugs like marijuana?"

I answered no again. The light made it hard. It gave everything an unrealistic quality. I told myself that I could get up and walk out the back door through the fields and climb down the bank. You could keep walking that way, all the way to the river.

Officer Townsend folded his hands on the table in front of him and leaned toward me a little. He had on a pair of glasses, and I saw how the light was reflected in them over and over. "Could you describe your relationship with David Sanderson? How long have you known him?"

My mother walked over to the table and stood just behind my chair. "They've known each other since they were four," she said. "You know that."

"It's better if Kay answers," Officer Townsend said, glancing up at her. "Were the two of you friends, Kay?"

"Yes," I said.

"Friends from childhood?"

"Yes." I stared down at my hands. They were dried out, I noticed, and one of the nails was torn back so far I told myself it must hurt.

"What kind of friends? Good friends or just sort of neighborhood friends?"

"Good friends," I said, looking up again, so that I was flooded with the light. "All three of us were good friends."

He stared at me for a moment, as if this piece of information was registering. "You mean, you and David and Michael were all three good friends?"

I nodded.

"What about more recently? Were you and David intimate physically?"

I closed my hands together, interlocking the fingers. It was a simple gesture, I told myself, not anything like prayer. "We started seeing each other this year, when I went to college."

I felt my mother touch the back of my chair. "The year before, when David went to live on campus, Kay was still in high school, and they hardly ever saw one another," she explained.

Townsend looked at her, pausing for a moment. "Ms. Richards," he said, and I remember thinking that it sounded oddly formal, "you're going to have to step back and let Kay answer." He glanced at the notes his partner had taken, and I felt my mother's hand loosen her grip on my chair, but she didn't step back.

"How often did you and David see one another while you were living on campus?" Townsend asked, turning back to me. "Was it daily or more like once a week?"

"Maybe five or six times," I answered.

"A week?"

"Yes." I focused on the table beneath my hands, noticing

how dark the wood was under the brightness of the light and how the grain stood out, along with the nicks and scratches in it.

"What did you do together five or six times a week?" He folded his arms, watching me calmly as I tried to think of how to answer.

"Did you go out together or leave campus? Did you spend time together in one another's room?"

I glanced up at him. "Yes."

"Yes?" We sat there for a moment, staring at one another. He closed his eyes for a second and then opened them again. "You did all those things?"

"Yes."

"And you had a sexual relationship?"

"I don't see why you're asking this," my mother interrupted. She had stepped away from the table and knocked something over on the stove. "It doesn't—"

"Ms. Richards," Townsend said, looking up impatiently at her, "you're going to need to step out of the room if you can't let your daughter answer the questions." He shifted forward in his chair, and I thought for a minute he was going to stand up. My mother turned toward the stove. I could see her picking up the teakettle and wiping away the water that had spilled. She carried it to the sink and rinsed it off.

"Was it a sexual relationship?" Townsend asked, looking back at me.

I looked past Officer Townsend, where the room was blinding with light. "No," I answered. "We were just going out."

"All right," he said slowly. "And last night, did you take the LSD with him before driving out to the bridge?"

"Yes." I said it softly, still looking past him into the light.

"At about what time?" My mother turned from the sink, and I could feel her watching me.

"I'm not sure."

Townsend shifted his weight, leaning back from the table. "How much did you take?"

"We each took one of the tablets," I said, carefully spreading my fingers out on the table, feeling the coolness of the wood underneath them.

"Where did the LSD come from?"

"David had it. I don't know where he got it from."

He glanced at the other officer. "Had David done any drugs before?"

"No."

"And afterward you went on a drive. Whose idea was that?"

"David said we should go."

"Where did you drive to?"

I closed my eyes, but the light was still there, as if it were lining the inside of my head. "We were in David's car, and we went on back roads around here. Michael wanted to go out to a main road and get something to eat, but David didn't want to drive out to the diner."

"This was about what time?"

"I'm not sure," I said, looking up at him again. "Close to midnight. Maybe eleven or so."

He pushed himself back from the table, signaling the other officer, who held down the notebook so that Townsend could read it. "Did you stop anywhere else before you got to the bridge?" he asked after a minute.

"We went by a railroad crossing," I said as Officer Sadoski took the notebook again. "The one near Routes Five and Ten."

"And you stopped there?"

I nodded. There was a basket of napkins on the table, and I took one suddenly and started folding it in my hands. "Yes."

"For how long?"

"Several minutes," I said, shrugging. "Maybe fifteen or so."

"Why did you stop there?"

"We were waiting for the train," I said, creasing the napkin deeply. "And after it went by, we left."

He glanced up again at Officer Sadoski. "Why were you waiting for the train?"

"I don't know. Just to see it."

"To see it." He tapped his fingers against the table. "All right. And where did you drive after that?"

"I'm not sure; we were on back roads. We went over the Sunderland Bridge at one point and then out to Millers Falls," I said, folding the napkin again, feeling the pinch of the crease under my fingers.

"And then you drove to the French King Bridge?"

"Yes."

"And where did you pull over?" He leaned toward me again, staring at the napkin, and I felt the crease I'd been making tear under my fingers.

"We stopped on the side of the road on the bridge."

"On the side that comes from Millers Falls?"

I nodded.

He leaned closer. "Whose idea was it to stop and get out?"

"It was David's," I said, crumpling the napkin in my hand. "Michael didn't want to."

"And what about you? Did you want to go out onto the bridge?"

"Not at first, but David wanted to go."

"Was there an argument?"

"No."

"Did any of this seem dangerous to you?" he asked, looking from my face to the napkin, which lay now on the table. "Driving while under the influence of LSD or stopping by the railroad tracks or on the bridge?"

I shook my head. "No," I tried to say.

"Excuse me?" He tapped the table just in front of me.

"No, it didn't. Not at the time."

He looked up at the other officer, signaling him again to lower the notebook so that he could see what had been written. "So the three of you got out and walked across?" he asked after a couple of minutes.

"Yes. Then Michael turned around and went back," I answered.

He knit his eyebrows together for a second, and in that light all the lines that had lain just underneath his skin surfaced. "Why did he go back?"

"I think it was because he was dizzy when he looked over. Maybe he was cold," I said, picking up the napkin again, shredding it.

"And you and David continued to walk out across?"

"Yes." I turned and looked for a minute at my mother. She

was still standing in front of the sink, and I could see where she had set the kettle next to it to dry. She was facing us, her arms folded across her chest.

"You stopped at the place you showed me last night, near the center of the bridge?"

I nodded.

"Tell us what happened next. What did David say?"

"That he wanted to jump off," I said slowly. "That we could swim to the side."

I looked up into his face and saw that the creases in it were hard and deep. "Did you understand what he meant?"

"Yes."

"Even though you were high?"

I glanced at my mother again. She had closed her eyes. "Yes."

"What happened next?"

I swept my hands across the table, and as the napkin dropped to the floor, I stepped on it, covering it with my shoe. "I don't remember. I guess he went over the rail."

"You don't remember?" He took the notebook then from Sadoski and put it on the table between us. "Think about it for a minute. Did he climb up? Did you help him at all?"

My mother moved toward us. Her arms were uncrossed now, her hands gesturing. "Can't you see she doesn't know? She's been hysterical off and on since last night."

"How did your arm and face get bruised?" He pointed to the area above my elbow that showed partway because of the sleeve. The bruise had spread, as if someone had wrapped his fist around my arm, and it was nearly black in all that light, with a fine outline of purple around the edges.

"I can't remember."

He stood up then and handed the notebook back to the other officer. He said something that I couldn't hear. "You can't remember?" he asked me again, stepping back toward the table.

"No," I repeated. "I don't remember."

He stood there for a moment, staring at the place on the table where the napkin had been. "All right," he said. "We're done. You need to look these over and sign this statement. It says you agree that what's written down here is what you told us."

I took the notebook and quickly wrote out my name.

"Wait a minute," my mother said as I handed it back to him. "Doesn't she need a lawyer present before she signs something?"

"Not really," Officer Townsend told her, taking the notepad from me as he walked to the door. "We're just trying to get a few facts. We have to write up a report about what happened, and this just says that what she's told us is true as she knows it."

After they left, I sat there for a long time, staring at the kitchen window. It was mid-March, and the trees hadn't flushed out yet. Everything was still bare, the ground covered with a scattering of dead leaves. At the back of the yard, where the thick brush grew, you could see the path that looped around to David and Michael's house.

Later my mother cooked and carried the food next door. I want to say I was sobbing, but I don't think I was. What I remember is a kind of numbness, the feeling of being detached. And when I fell asleep, it was sudden and deep and dreamless. My mother found me that way, "passed out on the living room couch," as she told me later. The kind of sleep that can be healing or can leave you feeling unsteady, as if you were gone for so long you're no longer sure of anything that's happened. My mother said she covered me with a blanket and kept the room dark. I slept so soundly it was more than a full day before anything woke me.

Kevin

I T ' S A L M O S T D A R K by the time I leave the bridge and start back home, and the air is gray and feathery, as if there might be things we can only half see between the trees. Almost five days now, and each evening the house is full of people—friends and neighbors, people we work with, and Ellen and Kay. As I come through the door, Jen pulls me into the dining room, the one place in the house that's empty. For the first time in what seems like years, I look around the room and see what's there—the windows with the deeply set wooden frames I painted the summer after we moved in, the faded lace tablecloth with a stain running down one side, and the chairs that need reupholstering. I picture David taking it over, the way he did when he was home for Christmas, spreading his books across the table and setting piles of papers on the various chairs.

"They're writing another article about it for the newspaper," she says. There's a light on in the room, and you can see the streaks of gray running through her hair mixed in with the strands of brown. It touches her shoulders when she leans her head back and runs her hand through it. I've been out at the bridge most of the day again, talking with the officer who was searching the shore and walking along it myself.

"Who's writing an article?" I ask her. There have been a couple of articles already, describing David's fall and the search that's been going on.

"His name is Timothy Bookman, and he wanted to know if he could interview us. The dean, Tom Merrick, phoned also. The newspaper contacted the university to ask if there was any evidence of a drug problem at school."

She presses her hands together, staring up into my face. I glance out into the hall. Eric, my department chair, is coming in through the front door with his wife, carrying what looks like a roast or a large lasagna.

"He's calling back," Jen says, and I feel her hand along the back of my arm. "Kevin." I turn around, stepping toward her. Eric is in the kitchen now. I can hear him talking with Jonathan and the sound of his wife laying out the food. "What are we going to say?"

She is staring at me, her eyes large, her lips drawn. I imagine pushing her back against the table and putting my hands under her clothes. I want suddenly to have her under me, where I never have to let go; I want to make David there between us, all over again.

"Why do we have to talk to him? Tell him we won't do an interview."

"If we don't, they'll say whatever they want." She drops her hand as she turns away. "I can't stand this anymore. It sounds like they're going to print all this stuff about him that isn't even true. 'We'd like to find out about your son's drug use and how you were dealing with it as parents.' That's what he said. They'll imply that he was involved in all kinds of drug use if we don't talk with them. I feel like I'm in this alone. You're out there constantly, and I have to make all the arrangements. I have to try to figure this out." She walks to the doorway, and I can hear more people coming in through the front entrance.

"I want you to talk to the reporter when he calls back," she continues. "I want you to give him a time to come by tomorrow when you'll be here, and we need to sit down beforehand and talk about what we're going to say."

"Jen." It's Sandy Turner, a veterinarian who works for the wildlife group that Jen also works for. I stand by the dining room table watching as she puts her arms around Jen, and I try to remember if I've touched her since we got the phone call five nights ago.

"I know, I know," Jen says, moving down the hall toward the kitchen now, away from me. "It's impossible to think of anything to say." And then, "No, Kevin's handling it. He's handling it in his own way."

When they're gone, I stand beside the door for a while and stare at the window with its off-white curtains. I try to remember when they were hung and if Jen made them or if I went with her somewhere to pick them out. Maybe the gulf that's between us was there even before anything happened to David. I can hear her voice coming from the other room with a kind of forced calm to it.

After a while Eric and Jonathan come in to talk with me and make more offers to cover my classes. "Take as much time as you need," Eric says. "Don't worry about the semester. Just get through this."

Jonathan puts out his hand as if he is about to lay it on my shoulder, but I step away, and he ends up patting the air. "We should get together sometime soon," he says, glancing at Eric. "Sometimes talking helps to put things like this behind you."

I lean against the doorjamb. I want to say this won't get put behind me, that I'm still out there looking, even when I'm here in my dated dining room. Down the hall I can see two of Michael's basketball buddies.

"Jen seems worn out," Jonathan comments. He looks past me, down the hall toward the kitchen, where Ellen is probably arranging food.

"Did you know about the drugs beforehand?" Eric asks. He stares at me for a minute, then lowers his eyes. His body looks relaxed with the slumped posture, hands in his pockets, but his face is lined with worry.

"No," I tell him. Jonathan is looking around the corner as if the conversation isn't taking place.

"It could be difficult, with you teaching at the university," Eric says after a minute or two of no one's saying anything.

I step out of the dining room, and the two of them follow me.

"Is Kay Richards coming back to finish the semester?" Eric asks, changing the conversation as we move toward the kitchen.

"I don't know," I tell him.

More of my colleagues are standing around in the kitchen, and I recognize several other people we know from around the area—a teacher from the high school who took an interest in David, a friend I've gone canoeing with, and a couple of parents whose kids are friends of Michael or David. Conversation is muted, but I think I hear a reference to the acid. Ellen hands me a plate with some roast on it. "I'm not hungry," I tell her. Then the phone rings, and Jen materializes, handing it to me.

"It's the reporter," she says. "You need to arrange a time to meet with him."

I take the phone from her and carry it into the hallway. "I'll meet with you tomorrow," I tell him, cupping my hand around the receiver and turning to the wall, lowering my voice. "But you have no business doing this."

He says he just has a few questions, that naturally people would like to know how it happened. "I hate to publish anything without your interpretation of it. This is something for other kids and their parents to talk about," he says. "It'll wake them up."

I start thinking about waking up and wondering if that's what death is like, not waking up anymore, not being able to pull out of the soup of your dreams.

"Is nine o'clock good?" he asks when I don't respond.

"No," I tell him, thinking that I want to go out to the bridge again early in the morning. "It'll have to be later."

"Then I'll meet you at your house at, say, eleven?"

When we hang up, I go back through the crowded kitchen again. Jen is in the family room now, where there are photographs laid out on the floor. Ellen sits with her, along with Sandy and three or four other women Jen is friends with.

"This print is great," I hear Sandy comment. "If you have the negatives for a few of these, I'll take them and get enlargements made for you."

Jen says she does have them somewhere, and Ellen offers to search one of the closets for a box Jen thinks they're stored in.

"We could also get enlargements made up from the prints," another woman tells her.

I stand in the room for a few minutes watching them hover. Ellen comes back with the box. She sits back down next to Jen and and takes the lid off the box, removing the photographs that are on top. I go over to where they're sitting and stare down numbly at the spread of pictures across the coffee table—David at eight, David at fourteen, at twenty, at three, black-and-white or glossy color images floating. "What are you doing?" I ask them.

"I'm trying to pick out some photographs," Jen says, looking up at me, the graduation picture in her hand. "We're going to have to plan some sort of service."

I shut my eyes for a second so that everything I see turns dark. "Not yet," I tell her, opening them again. "It's too soon."

"You heard what Greg said. They expect the body to turn up downstream. But even if it doesn't . . ." She looks back at the graduation picture, an eight-by-ten, and I see the tears in her eyes starting to form.

"I'll frame that one for you," Ellen says, taking it from her. "I'll make one for it."

It doesn't look like him—the combed hair, the flawless skin, or the shirt he wore that day and the tie. Jen is crying now, the women drawing around her. I go outside where it's a cold, clear night, the sky thick with stars. Our yard is over an acre, and it stretches back to a field that leads to the river, so it seems to go on forever. On one side it borders Ellen's property. Compared to Jen, Ellen is a large woman with wide hips and thick curling blond hair, her lion's mane as Jen calls it. I've watched her have relationships with different men. She lives an artist's life, staying up sometimes all night in her studio behind the house, creating unusual sculptures of clay. There's always been something exotic about her. Forty years ago she would have been considered voluptuous. At one point I know that Jonathan wanted to marry her, but she made it clear she wasn't interested in commitment.

I end up standing in the yard staring at her house and the field that goes down to the river until I'm cold. If I drove down to the bridge again, with no one there this late at night, I could walk out onto it and scream over the side. There's a part of me that's considered jumping ever since we heard, so that I'll know what he went through.

When I go back into the house, almost everyone has left, but I can hear Ellen and Jen in the kitchen, Ellen saying to drink the tea she's made while she finishes the dishes.

"I want to talk with Kay more about what happened," Jen says. "If David was doing drugs before that night, she would have known about it."

Ellen doesn't say anything, and for a minute or more there's just the sound of water being run into the sink and silverware hitting up against the stainless steel. "I don't want anyone to talk to Kay right now," she says finally. "She's too fragile."

Jen's chair moves back across the floor. Her cup scrapes against the table. "So am I."

They quit talking as I come into the room. "You look tired," Jen tells me, her face softening, her hand reaching out. "You should get some sleep if you can."

I walk past them to the other side of the room and glance down the hallway toward the front door. "Is everyone else gone?"

Jen nods. "I think Jonathan and Carl Kaufman are still talking on the front porch. Everyone else just left a few minutes ago. Michael went upstairs, and Kay went home."

"Are you going to see how Kay is?" I ask Ellen, hoping she'll quit the dishes and take off. There are things I don't need right now—the photographs of David spread across the house, the sound of her voice in the kitchen, the clean silverware and plates.

"In a minute," she says, turning the water on again.

I go out into the front hallway, where Michael is sitting in the dark on the stairway, and sink onto the step below him. For a while he stays there unmoving, his chin against the palm of his hand. Then he stands and goes up the stairs. Everyone is gone now, it seems, except for Ellen, who finally walks to the front door with Jen. I watch as they put their arms around each other before Ellen walks away. Then Jen stands there, looking out into the darkness. When she finally closes the door and turns toward the stairs, she still doesn't know I am there.

"That reporter, Timothy Bookman, is coming at eleven tomorrow," I tell her, clearing my throat.

"All right." She steps backward, startled. "I have to meet with the counselor at Michael's school. I should be back by eleven-thirty."

She looks at me, and I see how bloodshot her eyes are. "I'm going to bed," she says, and I feel her hand press into my shoulder. I suddenly remember the way she was in her early twenties, when she would stay up all night, past exhaustion working on something for a political campaign or animal rights.

As she goes up the stairs, I sit there listening to her feet brush against the carpet. I imagine the way the backs of her legs would look moving beneath the denim skirt. The door to the bathroom opens and closes. Several minutes later I hear her talking to Michael, her voice quiet and restrained. I'll eat what's left of the roast beef. Then I'll lie on the couch for a while in the family room where the photographs are spread across the table. Later, if I still can't sleep, I'll get in my truck and drive out again to the river.

TIMOTHY BOOKMAN IS young, probably in his early thirties with a nervous kind of eagerness, like a graduate student who is so anxious to write his dissertation he doesn't take enough time to do the research.

"How much did you know about your son's substance abuse?" he asks sitting in a chair facing me in the living room. "Are you aware of any other drugs besides the acid that he was taking?"

"There are no other instances of his being involved in any way with drugs," I tell him. "You do not get the kinds of grades David got if you are using drugs."

He passes the tip of his pencil across his mouth. "So he was a good student?"

"He had a three-point-eight last year," I state simply. "He was considering a premed major, but he was equally interested in the classics."

"Had he supplied drugs to anyone else besides Kay Richards?"

I stare at him for a moment, taking notice of the well-thumbed notepad balancing on his knee and the recorder he's asked if he can use with the tape spinning in it. "He was not supplying drugs to anyone," I say carefully. "He and Kay Richards had two tablets of acid. That's all we really know. They each took one."

He pauses, jotting something down in his notebook. "Are you saying Ms. Richards could have supplied it?"

I shrug, thinking that even though no one has mentioned this as a possibility, it *is* a possibility. "As far as I can tell, who supplied it is an unknown."

Changing the subject, he asks if I see a lot of drug use among the students at the university. "Would you say there's a drug problem? Or are you aware of any problems with drugs?"

I sit there, watching the tape turn, trying to slow the pace of my thoughts. "There are drugs on every college campus," I tell him. "But, no, I'm not aware of any severe drug problems."

He leans forward, and the notepad slides off his knees to the floor. "Were you aware, the night of your son's death, that he and his girlfriend had taken acid?" he asks as he bends over to pick it up.

"No. Of course not." I keep my voice even and force myself to sit back comfortably in my chair. "I would never have let them drive if I had known. That was reckless."

As soon as I say the word, I regret it. "Reckless?" he asks, his eyebrows lifting, his mouth working so that you can see the next question forming on his lips. "Would you say that—"

Just then the front door opens and closes, and I hear Jen come inside. She sets down whatever it is she is carrying and opens the hall closet, taking out a coat hanger and putting it back. Then she comes down the hall, pausing at the living room.

"Sorry I'm late," she says, reaching out to touch the door frame, steadying herself.

"That's okay." The reporter stands up. "I hope you'll join us. I have a few more questions, and I'd like your opinion as well."

While she goes into the kitchen to put on some coffee, the two of us sit there not talking. Bookman turns away to check his recorder. When Jen comes back, she settles herself carefully in the chair next to mine. "We were talking about David's behavior on the night of the accident," Bookman tells her, glancing at me. "Kevin commented that driving a car while under the influence of a drug like acid was reckless and that he hadn't known about it or he would have prevented them from taking the car."

Jen is thrown off balance. I can see it in the way her expression changes, her mouth opening and her chin jutting out. Then she turns to look at me for what seems like a full minute, as if I've betrayed her by some careless admission. "There was a party here that night," she says. "Things were pretty confused, with a lot of people coming and going. As a parent, you can't possibly know everything a teenager does."

Bookman makes another note in his pad. "So you were hav-

ing a party here that night when David and his girlfriend took
the acid?" he says, looking at Jen.

Jen nods. I can smell the coffee dripping through the filter. I
can almost hear it even this far away. Then the reporter mumbles
an apology about how hard this must be, to talk so soon after the
accident, and I start thinking about what a curious word "accident" is until it hits me the other thing it could be called is a
suicide.

"He'd never done anything like that before," Jen says, and
even though there aren't any tears in her eyes yet, I can tell she's
starting to cry by the catch in her voice. "I'm sure he was just
experimenting. He was responsible." Her voice wavers. "At his
age kids try out all kinds of things."

"What kinds of things?"

She glances at me. "I don't know. I mean, he had a car, one he
had saved for himself, and he liked to drive it all over." She stops
talking and looks down at the hands she's placed in her lap.
"What I meant is that you often read that kids this age will
experiment with different things like alcohol or drugs, things
they might not ever do again."

I watch her pull a Kleenex from her pocket and wipe one
of her eyes and the other cheek, wondering with half my brain
if that night *was* the first time he had used drugs; the other
half of my brain telling me it had to have been. The reporter lowers his voice and asks if David had ever tried taking anything else.

Jen shakes her head, still staring at her hands. "No," she says.

I clear my throat, folding my arms in front of my chest. "I
think what we're saying is that the onetime use of a drug by a
kid his age is not unusual."

"Oh." He raises his eyebrows a little and makes another note. Then he wants to know more about the party, how many people were here and whether or not there was alcohol.

"There were a few beers. Maybe a bottle of wine," I tell him, flashing for a second on what the kitchen counter looked like the next morning, still covered with bottles and remembering the noise that was coming from the family room when we started listening to some old recordings. Much of the night I stood on the deck arguing political theory with Jonathan and Carl and a couple of graduate students. It occurs to me that because of that, I didn't notice that David and Michael and Kay were going out.

"The party was small," I emphasize. "A few of my colleagues came over and several friends."

"What about your own college experience?" he says, glancing from me to Jen. "What year would that have been?"

"Late sixties," I tell him, fairly certain where he's headed.

"And naturally, there were drugs around then."

"Of course," I say, almost laughing. "Marijuana was widespread."

He shifts forward in his chair, pawing the notebook. "So do you think your own use or experimentation has made you more relaxed about your children's drug use?" he asks.

"No. I did not say that either of us took drugs. I was merely pointing out the ridiculousness of your question. And we were not relaxed as parents about drug use. As far as we know, with the exception of the onetime use of acid that night by David, there *was* none." I glance at Jen to see if she wants to confirm this, but she is staring straight ahead, her face dazed.

Bookman asks more questions about drug use on campus.

Then Jen gets up to check on the coffee, but by the time she comes back with it, he has already stood. "None for me, thanks," he says as he closes up his tape recorder. "I feel bad enough already to have taken this much of your time."

I walk with him to the door, but then, as I'm opening it, intent on saying something to him out of Jen's earshot about what he plans on publishing, the phone rings and Jen calls me. Timothy Bookman slides out the door, and as I turn toward the kitchen, Jen passes me the phone. One of the cups in still in her hand, and I notice that the coffee has sloshed out and spilled on the rug.

A man on the other end tells me he is with the coroner's office and that he believes they have David's body. "It was found in Barton's Cove by a couple of guys who had taken their boat out fishing."

"Fishing?" I ask, not comprehending.

"Yes."

When I get off the phone, Jen is standing in front of the sink running water over the cups. "I thought they wouldn't find him," she says.

I put on my jacket and wrap my fingers around the keys that are in the pocket. I'm operating on a kind of automatic pilot, and even this small gesture feels foreign, as if I am cut off. "You don't have to come with me," I tell Jen. "I can call you from the hospital and let you know if it's him. They'll need to do an autopsy, and we could decide what we want done with the body afterward."

But she turns toward the door, wiping her hands against her shirt. "I'm coming," she says.

The drive out there takes forever. It's warm, so I roll down my window. I repeat the information I've been given on the phone, trying to determine how we'll we handle things when we get there, but Jen doesn't say anything.

"We'll have to look for identifying features—hair color, height, shreds of the clothes he was wearing," I tell her. "They can still check his blood type, and we'll have to ask the dentist for his dental records. The man said they'll perform an autopsy. They can find out what drug he was on, and maybe they can determine the cause of his death."

The road is almost empty. Inside me there's a kind of horrible relief to be headed toward conclusion. "We know the cause of his death," Jen says after a while.

When we get to the hospital where the coroner's office is, I park and we go inside. There is preliminary paperwork and explanations of how things are run. Eventually we're taken into a room that looks a little like a doctor's examining office. It is cool and quiet inside the room, and there is a longish form on the table under a heavy piece of rubber or plastic.

Jen's face is white, her features frozen, and the coroner who has brought us back tells us that it may be difficult to recognize the body as it is bloated from being in the water. He asks if Jen is certain she doesn't want to wait in the other room. "Why don't you do that," I tell her.

"No," she says. "I want to see him."

The coroner nods. He pulls down a zipper, and the heavy plastic bag peels open. What we see as he lifts it away does not look like David. The thick, dark hair is still on the scalp, but parts of the face look almost scooped out, the eyes and the lips almost gone. There are areas where there is no skin.

The coroner explains that the appearance is normal for what

they see when they recover a body from the river. "Fish and other creatures sometimes eat away the soft-tissue areas." The coat and shirt are gone, and the denim jeans are ripped and pulled away from one thigh. There's an overwhelming stench, and through the rip in the jeans I can see a hole where the penis and balls had been.

Jen starts throwing up. I hear her by the door, trying to open it, and the coroner tells her to go down the hall, next door on the right. The flesh looks like clay, I realize, the raw gray color of the clay we find by the river.

"The height is a match," the coroner tells me, his gloved hand resting on the table. "And the hair color. Also the clothing."

"Yes."

"We'll check the blood type and his dental records. Do you recognize the chain that's around his neck?" He points it out.

It's a linked chain with several distinctive twists in it, and there's a ring on it. I remember when he came home wearing it at Christmastime. He said that Kay had given it to him. "Yes," I tell him.

"Are you making a positive identification?"

"Yes."

After we leave the room, there are more forms to fill out so that they can perform the autopsy. "When we're finished, you can arrange to have the remains picked up," he tells me.

We get back in the truck, Jen still looking pale. "I don't see how you could say it was him," she says, clutching her stomach.

"Jen, you could see his hair and the face. He was wearing a ring that Kay gave him. They're going to have to fill out a death certificate. I am not letting them put this down as suicide."

I drive away without saying anything else. Jen bends over on the seat, her back rising and falling as if she's sobbing. "Sometimes I hate you," she says after a while.

Then we ride in silence, and when we pull into the driveway, we sit for some time, not moving. "I can't believe it was him," Jen says again.

"No," I tell her, thinking absurdly that the water had him, that it ate him away.

She leans against the door. "I wish they hadn't found him," she says, pulling up on the handle so that it snaps open. Then she pushes against the door, and there's a moment where she looks at me as it swings open. Her nose and eyes are swollen and red from crying.

When she gets out, I'm left sitting there alone. I remember him the way he was three years ago, still awkward, having just come into his height, reading everything I recommended with an excitement that was contagious and discussing the ideas he came up with. That was the year he got nearly perfect scores on the SATs. The following year he got accepted at Brown, but he decided to go to the state university because of the scholarship they offered him and so that he could stay closer to home.

He wouldn't have taken the drugs without someone else's influence. He wouldn't have jumped off a bridge. I look at the trees along the river, their impossibly beautiful silhouettes. Once you're motivated by a moral imperative, there's a clarity of vision, similar to that which comes with historical perspective.

By the time I climb out of the truck and go into the house, Jen is upstairs and the shower's running. Under it, I can hear the sound of her sobbing. I tell myself I should go to her and think

of something to say, but when I open the door, the entire bathroom is so steamy—it's like entering a thick, white cloud—and
there is a steady rushing sound, as if we are underwater. She stops
crying when she hears me, but I can see the shape of her body
through the curtain, bent over itself, collapsed. When the boys
were little, sometimes I would find her like that, sitting or kneeling in the shower, exhausted, letting the water run over her.

Before I can stop myself, I've taken off my shoes and socks
and pulled off my pants, my shirt, my underwear. The air is so
full of water I can feel it against my skin, penetrating the inside
of my mouth and my lungs even before I open the curtain and
step up over the edge of the tub.

Jen moves forward. I could run my hand down the curve of
her back. I could bury my face in her. I step under the water,
and it falls like bright beads, the pale blue color of the tiles.
Without thinking about it, I move my hands across her stomach.
"Don't," she says. I kiss the back of her neck. "Leave me alone."

I'm pulling her toward me, gathering her in. The water
washes over us and down the sides of our faces and our chests
and backs and stomachs. I open my mouth so it fills my throat. I
swallow and swallow until any taste is gone and the only thing
there is, is water.

"Leave me alone," she says again, but she turns around and
presses her mouth against mine, not kissing, but there. David was
conceived while we were backpacking together in the Rockies,
totally idealistic still about the world, making love in a field of
wild lupines, the peak of a mountain cut against the sky.

When she lies down in the tub and opens her legs, I kneel in
front of her, sliding my hands along the inside of her thighs. The

water is everywhere, rising up along the sides of the tub. I don't think about David's body now. I'm pushing into her, under the water, and I can see her coming, the release that's in her face as if everything is done and we are starting over. The beads of water are ringed with color. There's a second where they hang suspended before they fall.

Afterward we dry ourselves off. It is almost three-thirty by now, and Michael, who has been in school all day, will be home soon. We'll tell him. Then we'll make arrangements for a cremation and the service. After that I'll meet with Greg Townsend. I want a thorough investigation into where David could have gotten the drugs, and I want to know exactly what happened when he was on the bridge.

Michael

THE MORNING OF the memorial service, I refused to get out of bed. "Michael, get dressed." My mother's voice was stretched out, high-pitched.

The house had filled with relatives, but I could sleep right through the noise that came from them downstairs. I could bury myself in it.

"Michael, I've brought you some orange juice."

"You have a suit to wear, don't you, Michael?"

"Is there a piece of artwork you want to put on the altar or something the two of you shared, something that represents what you shared?"

Explosives, I almost told them, or a sword. *I looked up to him,* written out on a piece of paper. *The way he did well in school, the way he was unafraid to go after something, even if it was something hard.*

My mother was wearing a skirt and jacket she bought at a store downtown the day before. "I have nothing even to put on for something like this." And my aunt had insisted on driving her.

"A change of scene. To get your mind somewhere else."

My mind was somewhere else—down at the bottom of the river. What I couldn't quit thinking about was how fast he was over. I remembered my father once saying that the idea of heaven was pretty far-fetched, and it occurred to me that it was, wherever he went.

Would you bring him back? I asked myself, like I was God, the way you would uncurl a stick of chewing gum and flatten it out. I thought about it for a few minutes, hesitating, David and Kay by the rail, his hand inside her clothes, the look that I knew was on her face.

"I've brought you some breakfast," my grandfather said, standing in the doorway to my room. "Food for strength and coffee to get you through the day."

"Not this one," I answered.

When my mother had told him about the acid, he said, "Young people do crazy things."

He set down the food next to where I was lying sprawled out with the pad of paper. "I couldn't think of what to say either," he said, and for a second I could feel the place underneath everything else in me where I would be crying. Then it was gone.

"Eat something first. Maybe we can put down a few words."

I wanted to tell him I didn't deserve anyone's being nice. *Give it up,* I wanted to say. *Give me up.* Instead, I ate the food he brought, ravenous suddenly, as if nothing could fill me.

By one-thirty, a full hour before the service, I was dressed in a suit my mother had found somewhere, and there was a sheet of paper folded over and stuck in the pocket of the jacket with a list of things I could read off. *Fishing. Canoe trips down the river. Play-*

ing cards with a flashlight on one of our beds at night. Ball throwing. The way he taught me how to drive.

This will be a royal pageant, I told myself with a sense of irony he would have appreciated. Put on the monkey suits. We've got everything but the body, which is too grotesque. Pictures blown up to bigger-than-life-size, people moaning and crying, everything but the coffin and a corpse.

Mom insisted that she and Dad and I ride over together, the three of us in the car, Dad sitting at the wheel staring straight ahead through the windshield and Mom turned to the side window, crying. If I were David, I would have come up with something slightly offbeat to say, something humorous enough to get a smile, but full of depth and feeling. "He was magical," I'd heard Mom tell Grandpa the night before. "He always had the right words."

He had the right words that night all right, I started thinking. When we got in the car, he had insisted on driving. *"Whatever I do is intentional. I'm one hundred percent operable,"* he kept telling us.

"He made a real mess this time," I said out loud, not checking myself.

My mother turned a little in the seat, her face hollow-looking, her eyes red from the crying. "You need to try to hold yourself together," she said.

I got a mental picture then of me pressing the edges of my suit jacket together, as if whatever I was inside of myself could spill out into the car. Maybe drowning was like that—the water wearing away the surface of the skin until the organs and the muscles spilled out. Maybe death was like that—the dissolving of boundaries.

We drove through the center of town and pulled into the parking lot next to the church. Inside, the room was filling up. There were neighbors, kids we grew up with, several of the teachers from the high school and elementary school. There was Kerry and Sharon Mahoney, two girls he went with his junior and his senior year, and there was Cheryl, a girl he brought home for dinner last year from college. And others I didn't know.

Slowly, we went up to the front pew, where my grandfather and aunt were already seated. Around the altar was a display of photographs. The recent picture of David that had been blown up to poster size was propped on an easel. His hair was shorter than it had been in the last several months, buzzed a little on the sides, just long enough on top to hang down to the middle of his forehead. He was looking straight into the camera, smiling a lopsided half grin, his eyes dark and severe, as if underneath any joke he might make he was dead serious.

Flowers had been placed on the altar, vases of tulips and daffodils—no professional arrangements, as if everyone knew my mother's dislike of florists. The rest of the out-of-town relatives slid into the pew next to my grandfather. Then Kay and her mother came in and sat down in the one behind us. Someone played a Bach prelude, a favorite of my mother's. David wasn't the type to have had a favorite song, lyrics he had memorized. He had been able to play Mozart by ear when he was seven, but he'd never seemed to really listen to music much. It got to me, thinking about that, how he liked it quiet when he was working, how he seemed akin to silence.

"We're here to celebrate a life and mourn the passing of it," the minister began, which was when I made the connection, with David's picture up there, larger than life on the easel, like he was a king. I thought about all the time my mother had spent looking through the photographs and how she had talked about getting some of his writing together and publishing a book, as if she were making him into a legend.

After that, I couldn't get the worship motif out of my head. "As in life, he is with us in death." Worse than in life, I thought.

There was more music, and then people were asked to come forward and say something about him. A few of his teachers walked to the front and talked about his being a gifted student driven by inspiration, a model for us to aspire to. Then his friends from the high school and a bunch of them from the college came up. Some of them talked about him, but most of the girls just walked up and left something in front of the altar without saying anything. After a while there was a large pile of books and drawings, pieces of paper with things written on them, and more flowers. Next to me, my parents were crying.

When my grandfather got up, he took the piece of paper I had folded in my pocket and read from it. I sat there listening, remembering everything I hadn't put down, like the times we had talked late into the night, the flashlight under a tent of blankets, how he used to do magic tricks with a deck of cards and invent stories we acted out, and the times we had fought, like when we beat each other up in the front yard two summers ago until my mother's screaming made us stop.

When I started crying, the tears felt hot and grimy, and something in my head was screaming like it was about to explode. Then my mother got up and walked to the front of the church. She stood there for a moment, facing us, and when she started talking, her voice was so quiet it was hard to hear it. She told what David was like when he was little, how he would climb anything, how she found him once on top of the refrigerator. She described the two of us as always together, fishing and swimming, and how David taught himself the constellations and built contraptions with wheels and pulleys that filled the barn. She talked about him until my head was so full it throbbed. I put my hands on either side of it, like I could stop the heat or squeeze it out.

When she sat down, again the church was quiet. Then, before the minister could walk up to the altar, Kay stood up. She walked to the front, moving slowly. She didn't say anything, but she set down a sheet of paper and something small and gleaming. As she turned to go back to her seat, I saw that it was the ring that she had been wearing.

Afterward, I wanted to pound my head until it split. My father looked blank, like what was inside him had been scooped out. My mother put her hand through mine and led me to the car. People in the parking lot were standing around, waiting to follow us back to the house. Then, for a second, David poured into me, as if what he was now was all liquid and he could fill me up, the sense of him when he would laugh, when he would cuff me, kidding around in the yard. Like he was saying, *This isn't for real, man. What you know is that I'm right here.*

That feeling of him was cool, like the wind, but when it was gone, the throbbing heat rushed back, and I wanted to scream at him, *Asshole! You jumped off the damn bridge!*

"He thought he could do anything," I said when we were in the car. "He thought he could swim across the fucking river."

"Michael." My mother was crying silently, the tears squeezing out of the corners of her eyes, following the lines of her face.

"What did you mean by that?" my father asked, turning around in the seat. "What did you see that night?"

I stared out the window. Kay was getting into their car with her mother. She had something in her hands, a tissue or a scrap of paper, and she was tearing it to pieces. "They were having sex by the railing," I said, without thinking of what was coming out. "Then she helped him climb up onto the rail. He stood up like he was trying to balance."

"What are you talking about? Did she push him?"

Kay pulled the door to the car shut. I could see Ellen starting the motor. "Michael, you said she helped him onto the railing. Did she push him off it?"

"I'm not sure. I think so."

We sat there for a moment, with my father staring at me across the back of the seat, but he didn't say anything else. Most of the people were in their cars by now, and they were waiting for us to pull out. Then he turned around again and slowly put the car in gear.

When we reached home, I stayed alone in the car while they got out to open the house. My body was slick with sweat. I tried to get through to myself about what I had said—Kay might have pushed him off the bridge. It was what I had seen, the two of them sharing some strange kind of closeness. Maybe they had always had that between them, even when we were kids and I had thought it was the three of us together.

Cars pulled into the driveway and parked by the road. Someone opened the car door, my grandfather telling me to come inside, the eyes of my father following my movements as I walked into the kitchen. He would ask me again, and I knew already what I would say. Because her hands were on his thighs as he climbed onto it, because I couldn't stand how her hands were on his thighs, and she had leaned forward, into him as he fell from the railing.

Later, when the rooms were crowded with people, I put it away from me.

"He was always good at telling a joke," someone said.

"Mischievous."

"Exciting. He did the unexpected."

"He was smart," the high school English teacher commented. "He was always smart."

My mother drew me into her, holding me against her. "We loved him, Michael," she said. "And that's enough."

It surprised me in a way, the number of people who were there in our house. It seemed like they kept coming, many of them friends of David from around here and guys he had roomed with in the dorm, plus several girls who kept wiping their eyes. He always had lots of friends, while Kay and I were more solitary. That got to me, too, thinking about how other people loved him.

Kay was walking through the rooms crying, not seeing anything, and the comfort was in me again, the wanting to go to her and whisper something. When I saw her going out the back door, I followed her.

"Kay wait," I called, but she was already at the edge of the yard, running toward the field. "Wait up."

The sun by then was yellow and huge, the way you would

draw it with crayons when you were a kid. Kay didn't turn around or slow up any. "Kay, wait the fuck up. Where are you going?" I ran so fast I almost ran straight through her.

For a while I followed, without her answering. The trees along the path were budding, and the ground was spongy and damp. As we got close to the river, there were deep mud holes, and the bushes were full of birds.

"I can't believe he's dead," I heard myself saying when we finally stopped under the trees next to the water.

The river was churned up, moving fast. She was crying softly, trying to choke it back. She turned to look at me, and I saw how streaked her face was, the little bit of eye makeup she'd been wearing smeared, her skin reddened.

"I kept telling myself that he made it and they just hadn't found him."

She stared out across the river for a minute, then back at me, but it was like she wasn't seeing anything.

I'd imagined it a hundred times by then—the fall, the explosion of water when he hit the surface, how cold it would have been, how it must have rushed into his mouth and nostrils, pinning him. "They think the body was caught for a while in some of the debris under the bridge. It could have happened before he was even drowned."

"Stop it." She was sobbing now, without any sound, bent over herself, the dark, curling hair on her narrow shoulders. "Stop."

"Stop," I almost said, mocking her. But I had my hands on her head, I was sinking them into her hair like I could shake her loose.

"He was fucked up!" I yelled at her. "He thought he could

do anything. The perfect son, the perfect student. He could swim across the goddamn river in the spring at night. He could jump off the damn bridge."

I had her head between my hands, and I pulled a piece of the silken hair from her face.

"No," she said.

"No what?" I wanted to kiss her suddenly. I wanted to smash her head against the bank. "No, he didn't *think* he was perfect? Or no, he actually *was* perfect?" She pulled away from me, sobbing loudly. "You did think that he could swim it, even though the water was freezing, even with the damn current." I leaned over, holding her arms to the ground, my legs on her legs, my weight, like when we were kids, I thought suddenly, and it cut through me, the way we would wrestle on the ground.

"He could swim. He went all the way across when the water was up. He—"

"He jumped off at night, Kay. When the water was freezing and from over a hundred feet up." Her face was wet and red. I put my face against hers. I wanted to say that we didn't stop him, that I knew he was high and I never tried to stop him. But I couldn't, and the fact of that stretched over us. He jumped, and we could have stopped him.

I opened my mouth and felt it against her, the way her skin was salty and warm. Dead was a long time, I was thinking, absurdly. Dead meant out of the picture, permanently. It meant a reconfiguration.

Kay started clinging to me. I could feel the shift in her body as it softened. "When you're older, we'll have to watch out,"

our mother used to joke. "She'll fall in love with one of you."
Like that would be the prize, I thought now ironically.

I lifted myself off her and peeled away the skirt she was wearing. "I should have jumped," she said. "I told him I would
jump."

"No." I pulled off her underwear, and it was wet and cold.
"You would have drowned also."

Under me, she was warm, her hair streaming through the
matted leaves on the ground. She had her eyes closed, the way I
was kissing her, the way I had her face between my hands again,
her legs under mine. And it was not like with Carolynn Miller,
at her parents' house with no one home and both of us groping.
It was natural and huge, like something outside of us was driving
me and I didn't have to think what to do next.

I shoved my pants down my legs. I opened her, and then her
arms were around my neck and I was grinding her into the
ground.

Afterward I stood and pulled on my clothes. I looked out
over the river again and saw how dark it was, moving fast. "We
should go back."

When I turned around, she had gotten up and was pulling on
her clothes. She was halfway up the bank when I picked up our
jackets and wadded the underwear she'd left into one of my
pockets.

We walked back to the house quickly, without talking. "Kay,
I was looking for you," her mother said when we came inside.
"What happened?"

Almost everyone had left by then. I followed her into the
family room, where a couple of David's friends were still sitting

with my dad. On the table were pictures of David and the things people had left at the church, like everything he was could be folded flat and fit into a drawer.

"I have to get out of here," Kay whispered. "We could drive over to the dorms and stay in my room."

"I can't," I told her, cold like a stone. "I have to go upstairs."

I turned away and walked partway up the steps, then sat down holding on to the rail. Beneath me, the last few people were leaving. When Kay and her mother came to the door, my mother hugged Kay's mother. Next she put her arms around Kay, her lips pressing against Kay's cheek. Kay glanced at me, a dried leaf stuck to her jacket, clinging. Then there was this moment where she was following her mother through the door, and I knew everything was over, and I wanted all of it back.

PART THREE

Michael

K AY'S HAIR WAS long and feathery, like hundreds of tiny springs. Sometimes, when we were little kids, I wanted to brush it. "Get the tangles out," my mother would tell me, but there were too many of them, nested in layers. When she was in high school, she wore it just below her shoulders, like a dark cloud. She was more remote by then. Sometimes I would notice her watching me while I played ball on the driveway, and then I would dunk the ball hard or go in for a jump shot, imagining the slow smile and a look of admiration that probably wasn't there.

"Shoot, Michael!" I'd hear her yelling at my games. Or just my name, repeated, as she sat in the bleachers with David or my parents, ignoring the other players. She hated the cheerleaders. Sometimes I think she despised most of the student body. She did not fit into the small-town high school even more than David and I didn't fit in. She was like her mother that way. You looked at her and you knew she was different.

In the summer, when everyone else was down the road at the

Hartmans' pool, she would lie in her backyard, sunning on a lounge chair with her music going. I remember goofing around with the basketball or at the edges of the yard, just so I could get a look at her. From our yard you could see the way her swimsuit fit. You could read the letters printed on the baseball cap she had on. There would be a tall glass of iced tea and a bottle of suntan lotion on a table next to her.

"Let's get the hose," David told me one afternoon, appearing from nowhere. The hose lay on the ground at the side of the house, coiled next to the faucet. "She is the object of loveliness," he was singing out.

We crept closer, and within minutes I was laughing uncontrollably. When I peered over at her, I could see where the top of her suit ended, just under her breasts, and I kept going over that edge in my head until it felt like I'd run my finger there.

The suit was blue-and-white plaid, with shorts that were cut high around her legs and came up to just under her navel. The small clasp at the back of the top was made of clear plastic, and I imagined undoing it as we were pulling out the hose and testing the water.

She had a book, and David wanted to know what she was reading.

"Who cares?" I told him. I couldn't stand the suspense. I wanted to be next to her chair when it happened, like the prank was just an excuse to get near her.

"Hemingway," he said after a few minutes, squinting. "Soak the book, too."

I was the one who got sent back to turn on the faucet while David held the nozzle. *Give me the hose,* I thought about saying when I was next to the house again, but he had already reached the tree closest to her yard and was turning around, his arm in the air.

"Go," he hissed. I opened the valve all the way while he was running across her lawn, the sprayer held high. There was an arch of water, white and frothy. Then Kay raised the book over her head and winged it across the yard so that it landed by the door of her house, behind a bush.

"Ummm. Nice," she said, stretching out her legs and raising her arms over her head.

I was standing next to David, laughing like an idiot. There was a soft nest of hair under her arms, and with her arms raised like that, I could see part of her breasts. I saw the tan line where she changed color. I tried to picture her nipples rising in the center of the paleness, a darker pink, maybe lavender.

"Wonderful. Delicious." She turned over in the chair so that the spray hit the long length of her legs, the tiny shorts, and the smoothness of the skin on her back.

"Ahhhh." She sighed, breathing it out so the sound lasted forever. "That feels so good and cold." She rolled over again, and the spray hit her in the face. The water ran down her nose and over her lips.

David stood there for a full minute or more, like he didn't know what to do with the sprayer nozzle and all that water, since Kay was not screaming bloody murder or trying to grab the hose and turn it on us.

"Mikey!" he shouted suddenly as he spun toward me. The blast hit my chest, exploding, running down my shorts and up into my nose.

"The dancing man!" he jeered as I jumped into the air, my limbs doing all crazy things.

Kay was laughing also, sitting on the side of the lounge chair. I could see her through the spray of water smoothing her wet hair back behind her ears, tossing it forward and wringing the water from it.

After a few seconds I was on him like I was crazed, fighting for the hose. I felt the hollowness of his chest under my fists. The water was going straight up, over all of us.

"Yeow! Quit! You're nuts!" David wrapped his hands around my wrists. He shoved me, but I wouldn't go down.

Kay was out of the chair now, her hand on my arm, the other one around my fingers that held the hose sprayer. I could feel the heat from her body, and I was thinking she was like an engine to make so much warmth inside the coldness of the water.

"Let go," she said.

I released it, backing away from them, and as I did, David spun toward me.

"Dirt scum, dirtsucker!" The water hit me again full force in the face. "Water rat!"

I could hear Kay laughing, could see her face, her mouth wide open, the straight rows of teeth where the braces had just come off. Then I doubled over and ran toward our house.

"Coward!" David yelled as the arch of water spread higher so that I was covered by it even when I got back into our yard by the maple tree.

Mom was coming out of the barn. She glanced at the spray of

water as if it were nothing but a sprinkler, a watering that the yard needed.

"You're soaked," she said, stating the obvious.

"No kidding. Guess how?" I asked her.

"Get changed, wise guy." She reached up and rubbed my wet head.

Later, when I came back outside, I could see them together in her backyard talking. Kay had on shorts now and a T-shirt, and they were standing next to the fence where the roses were. I picked up the basketball and pounded it over and over against the side of the garage. Then I got on my bike and rode it three miles to Aaron's house, where Shawn and some of the others on the team had gotten together for a pickup game.

"Kay hated the water," David told me later, after we had eaten supper and were standing around in the kitchen with the dishes Mom had told us to wash. "She just acted that way to get us."

"You turd," I started to say. But I let him put his hand on my arm and shove me into the counter.

WHEN THE POLICE questioned me again, the day after the memorial service, I was in zombie mode. The night before, after everyone had gone, my father had come upstairs to grill me. "What were you doing outside with Kay?" he wanted to know.

I was sitting on my bed with my legs stretched out, staring at the wall. "Nothing. We went for a walk."

He stood there in the doorway to my room as if he had accusations but no clear place to go with them. "What do you mean, a walk? Where did you go?"

None of your business, I said to myself, but to him I said nothing.

He put his hands on his hips, and his voice lowered. Passive resistance was always the thing that got to him. "Michael. Tell me where you went."

I glanced up at him. "I told you. I went for a walk. I'm not in the mood to talk about it right now."

"What do you mean, you're not in the mood?" He crossed the room with a few long steps and stood over the bed. "You act as if all this is at your say-so, according to your convenience, when—"

"Christ, Dad, we just had the service for him."

He had stopped midsentence, and his mouth still hung open. "I just want to know what was going on with her," he said after a few minutes, lowering himself onto the end of the bed.

I folded my knees toward my body and dropped my face onto them. "She was upset after the service. So was I."

He looked down at the floor for a minute. Then he looked up and saw my coat flung over a chair next to the foot of the bed. "What's this?" he asked and reached over, pulling Kay's underwear out of the pocket. "Jesus Christ. They're Kay's, aren't they?"

We sat there for a moment, both of us staring at the underwear. It was skin-colored and bikini-shaped, with a band of lace around the top. There were marks where the ground had dirtied it. "Michael, did you have sex with her when you were out there?"

I shrugged.

"Did she come on to you?"

"I'm not sure how it happened."

He had wadded the underwear into one hand, clenching it inside his fist, and he leaned over so that his face was close to mine. "You're not sure?" he said bitterly, and I could see the way his mouth formed the words, as if they had a taste to them. "She was David's girlfriend. She was with him when he fell off that bridge. You just told me earlier today that you think she pushed him."

"I have no clue, all right? We've known each for forever. We went down to the river, and we were both upset. It just happened." There was a crack in my voice, and I watched him tighten his fist around the underwear, then drop it onto the floor.

"Have you ever done this before with her?'"

"No."

"I can't believe she came on to you right after the memorial service."

"She didn't come on to me," I said, dropping my face into my knees again. "I'm not sure how it happened."

"Did you rape her?" I looked up, and he was staring at me almost calmly, as if that would be conceivable.

"No. It was both of us. Afterward she wanted me to come back to her dorm with her and spend the night."

He glanced down at the floor where the underwear lay, crumpled, then looked back at me. "And what did you say when she asked you?"

"I said no. I'm sitting right here, aren't I?" I was crying now, but I didn't know it, the way sometimes it can all slide down the back of your throat at first. I was thinking how stupid I had been.

My father put his hand on my leg. "You have to tell me what you saw on the bridge."

"I already told you."

"You said they were having sex by the rail."

"I don't know," I said, still talking into my knees. "That's what it looked like."

"How do you mean it? Did they have their clothes partway off?"

"No, but David had his hands inside her clothes."

"Did she decide she didn't want them there? Was she pushing him away?"

I swallowed hard and made myself stop crying. "No, I already told you. It was like they were having sex."

"All right." He took his hand away and sat there for a moment, and I could feel him just sitting there.

"Then David got up onto the rail?"

"Yes." I turned away onto my side. There was a cold thing deep in me now, and it could go on forever, worse than the crying, a darkness about what I had done with her by the river, a self-loathing.

"Michael, you said earlier that you thought she pushed him."

"Leave me alone, all right? Just leave me alone."

I lay like that for a long time, not crying, but sunk into myself. After a while he got up and went downstairs.

"It's okay," he said before he left. "I'll take you in tomorrow to talk with Officer Townsend, again." Later, when I looked, I saw that he had taken Kay's underwear with him.

The next morning, when he came out to tell me that we had to drive over to the police station, I was out on the driveway shooting the basketball. The week before any of this had happened, I had gone up to Bard College to meet with the coach about playing there next year. He had come down to one of our games that winter and seen me play. While I was there, he'd told me he would get back to me in the next couple of weeks to let me know what kind of financial package he could get for me. Since then it had been all I'd thought about. Now I just dribbled the ball around and shot, not caring.

"I phoned Shawn's father, and he said to come over," my dad told me, walking out onto the driveway and reaching for the ball.

I ducked around him and laid the ball in. Then I dribbled it back deep and shot. The ball hit nothing but net.

"We need to go on over there." He walked toward me, and I drove around him again, putting it in with a scoop shot. He had made me say it, I was thinking, in those moments right after the service when everything was so raw and confused. I didn't know anymore what I had seen or if you could actually be sure about something like that. I didn't know why I'd said it.

"Michael." He stepped in front of me as the ball rolled away into the grass. "This is not a game."

Yes it is, I told myself. It's a goddamn, fucking game.

"Pick up your coat and get into the truck." He pointed to the denim jacket that lay in the dirt at the edge of the driveway.

I glanced at the house. Earlier my mother had been in the

kitchen. She and Kay's mom were best friends. Once I had complained that my mother told Kay's mom everything. "You're right," she'd admitted. "We're each other's confidantes." Today she had been quiet all morning, cooking something and taking care of the cat she'd adopted. I was guessing she didn't know anything about this.

My father walked over to the truck and unlocked the door. "All right," I told him, reaching down and grabbing my jacket with one hand. "You won."

When we were driving along the road, he asked if I knew what perjury meant. "It's a crime to lie when you're questioned by the police," he continued when I didn't answer. "Even if you're trying to protect someone." I was looking out the window. The sky was darkening, like it was going to rain. The field was full of crows, hundreds of them, and as we went past, they rose all at once like a blanket.

"I know that, Dad," I said, thinking that anything I said would be a lie if it wasn't what he wanted me to say. "I don't need you to give me a lecture."

"Just tell them what you told me," he said a few minutes later.

When we got inside, Officer Townsend, who was Shawn's dad, and a woman officer took me down the hall into a small room with a table in the middle of it and a few chairs. "You can wait out front, Kevin," he told my father. "Or if you want to go home, I'll drive him back for you afterward."

My father stood in the doorway to the room. He turned to Shawn's dad. "I want to be in there."

"I think it would be better if we had a few minutes alone with him." Shawn's father glanced at me. When I was younger, he had helped coach the youth basketball team I played on for a few years. I owed him for helping me with my jump shot and some defensive footwork.

My father backed down the hall, motioning to Shawn's father. "What's up Greg?" I heard him ask. Shawn's father said something about a few minutes alone being best and voluntary cooperation. Then he came back and opened the door to the room then, and I went in. I could still see the way my father was standing out in the hallway, wondering if he would able to get out of me everything that was said later.

I sat down in one of the chairs, and the woman officer pointed out a tape player. She asked if it was all right if they taped the interview. The lighting overhead was harsh, and the walls needed painting.

"Your father said you had some time to think about what happened and you remembered more of it," Shawn's dad said.

I nodded. I was thinking about Kay again and how warm her hair had been in my hands and how my body had simply moved into hers beyond anything I could think about doing or plan out. "Animalistic" was a word that occurred to me. "Primitive." How could you want someone that much and hate them all at once?

"Let's start with what you knew about your brother's relationship with Kay Richards. Did you know he was seeing her?"

"Yeah, I knew," I said slowly. Shawn's dad sat there for a moment watching me. He had a quiet way about him that made your thoughts slow down. He was like that when he was coaching also, watching more than talking to us from the sidelines, not yelling the way most coaches did.

"What did you know?" he asked after a few minutes.

I stared at the table. I had known all along. Even when we were kids, I had known. "They'd been going out together since the fall," I told him. "But Kay liked him when they were in high school. They didn't exactly go out together then, but she liked him."

"You felt that she had liked your brother for some time?"

I glanced up at him, nodding. "She used to get upset if he went out with someone," I told him.

"Anything else? Did you ever see them together?"

I shook my head, shrugging. "Not really."

"What about the afternoon when they came home for spring break and took the LSD? Could you tell they were involved? Did they act differently at all?"

I looked at him for a moment, not answering. His face was worn, and his hair was getting gray. I remembered how he used to have us all form a circle before a game. Then he would tell us in his quiet voice about how we had to function as a team. He'd say the same words every time about how each of us was part of something greater, the thing we made together. "Why do you do it that way every time?" a kid asked him once.

"Rituals help you focus," he said.

"Michael, did they act different at all the afternoon they came back for spring break?"

I nodded. "They were all over each other."

"All over? You mean touching one another?"

"Yeah." I sank down into the metal chair. Saying it made me feel sick inside. "They had their hands all over one another, and they kept making out."

He smiled a bit like he was sympathetic. "So you were sort of a third wheel?"

"Right." I heard myself laugh a little, snorting. "Sometimes, when they were still in high school, David would go out with someone else or he'd go to a party to see a girl, and Kay would get upset, and she'd want me to go with her over to the party or help her find him."

"And did you?"

I almost laughed again. I felt giddy suddenly saying this, like it was a relief to be running at the mouth. "Once she sat in the car in the driveway while I went inside Sharon Mahoney's house. David was at a party there, and Kay knew Sharon liked him. All the kids in there knew why I was saying for David to come out with me, and he acted cool, like he was a prize they were fighting for."

Shawn's dad looked over at the other cop for a minute, like he had no idea where to go suddenly with all I was telling him. I told myself to shut up. Maybe it was either tell nothing or tell everything. Maybe what I needed was a muzzle. "So she was jealous when he was with another girl?" he asked me.

"I guess," I told him, shrugging my shoulders.

"Was she jealous that night?"

I shrugged again, looking past him out the window, where it was even darker now and you could see that the wind had started to blow, bending the trees. "I don't know."

"Did she say anything that indicated she was feeling that way?"

"No."

He shook his head, like I'd completely messed him up. "But

the two of them were close physically while you were driving around?"

"Yes."

Then the woman officer leaned toward me, putting her hands on the table. "How did that make you feel?" she asked, and something far inside of me cracked. I thought, She knows what I did with Kay last night. "Did it make you nervous or upset?"

"Sort of."

"It must have made you uncomfortable," Shawn's father said as he shifted around in his seat.

"Were you jealous?" the woman asked me.

I looked down at the table. Yes! I felt like screaming at her. Everything with Kay was one big mess. "I guess," I said finally.

She leaned in a little closer to me. Her uniform was crisp like it had just been pressed, and she seemed young. She seemed like she knew whatever you were thinking. "That night, was there any kind of arguing that went on between you and David? While you were driving around or once you stopped on the bridge?"

"I thought we should go back home. I wanted him to let me drive."

"And how about once you were on the bridge? Did you argue with him then?" she asked.

"I told them I was going back to the car." She sat there watching me, waiting for me to say more. I remembered how I had yelled *"Screw you."* Then Shawn's father, Mr. Townsend, got up. He pushed his chair back under the table and walked over to the tape player and switched it off. "We'll be back in just a minute," he said, signaling the woman to go with him.

While they were gone, I sat there staring out the window. I was jealous. Maybe anything I did was because I was jealous. Outside, clouds were still massing. It looked like the air was so full of water you could see the drops in it even though the rain hadn't started yet.

When they came back into the room, Shawn's father asked me if I wanted anything to drink. "No," I told him. "I'm fine."

The woman officer turned the tape player back on. She sat down again next to it and put a notebook on the table in front of her, like she was another recorder. Shawn's father folded his hands, resting them on the table. It wasn't until later that I thought about what might have been said between them. "So that night at the party and later, when the three of you were driving around, did it seem like Kay and your brother were getting along?" Shawn's father asked me.

"Sure," I said.

"How did you realize that? Can you think about how they were acting around one another? You said they were all over each other. Was there anything else?"

"Kay agreed with whatever David suggested, if that's what you mean."

He nodded. "What did she agree to?"

"I don't know. Taking the acid with him. Riding in the car." Everything, I thought. She had smiled at him constantly, like whatever he did or said was golden.

"Those were his ideas?"

"Yes."

The woman wrote something down on the paper in front of her. "Do you know who supplied the acid?" she asked me.

"Kay said that it was David's."

Shawn's father looked at me. "Did you see him give it to her?"

"No," I said. "I didn't."

"What happened after you stopped on the bridge?"

"They walked out along the walkway to the middle and then I turned around and went back to the car. I was pissed because they wouldn't come with me."

"They were standing at the middle of the bridge, the point where he fell, when you got into the car?"

"Yes." We sat there for a moment with him just watching me, the way he sometimes would at a game, quiet and accepting, as if whatever you did would be okay, whether it was the right or the wrong play. And it got to me, him watching me that way when I didn't know anymore what was the right or the wrong play. I got up from the chair and went over to the window. It had started to rain, large, slow drops at first that spattered against the glass, then faster and heavier until you couldn't see past the streams of water.

"What happened, Michael, after you got back in the car?" Shawn's father asked.

I kept staring out the window, trying to see the coffee shop that was across the street that we used to go to, but the rain was so thick you couldn't see anything. "The key was on the seat," I told him. "I put it in the ignition, but it didn't start right away. I was fiddling with the key, trying to get it to start, and then I looked up. They were at the edge of the bridge, against the railing. They had their arms around each other, kissing."

I turned and looked back over at the table where Shawn's

father and the woman were sitting. I could see that the tape recorder was still turning. "What happened next?"

"They were fooling around."

"What do you mean, fooling around? Were they kidding around, being silly?"

I shook my head and looked out the window again at the water. "Fooling around sexually."

"How?"

"David had his hands under her shirt and inside her pants." I stepped toward the window and touched the glass.

"Did Kay look like she wanted David to stop?"

"No," I said quietly. "She didn't want him to stop."

"What happened next?"

I took a breath, and it was like everything went out of me, and I thought, I hate them both, but then I couldn't feel anything at all. "He got up onto the rail."

"Did he climb up onto it?"

"I think so." It was thundering not too far away, the large crack and then the rumbling.

"Was Kay still touching him?"

"She had her hands on his legs like she was helping him up there. Maybe they were still fooling around." I looked out the window again. Through the rain you couldn't make out the street or even the tree just beyond the window. You couldn't see much but the water.

"Michael, it's important to remember the details," Shawn's father said slowly. "How were her hands placed on him?

I could picture them, Kay standing behind him with her shirt hanging open where it had come undone, the shiny white material of her bra, and David crouching on the rail facing the water. "She was holding on to him the whole time," I said. "She had her hands on his body while he was crouching on it, and then, as he stood up, she held on to his legs."

"Where on his legs?"

"She was reaching up and holding on to his knees."

"Did she push him or lean against him in any way?" Shawn's father asked immediately.

I could hear the rain, the drops smaller now, like a dance. "That's what it looked like. Her body was leaning that way."

"Was she pushing him away sexually?" he wanted to know. "What was she doing as he fell?"

But something in me had clammed up, shut tight.

Later it was impossible to take it back, even though the more times they asked me, the more uncertain I became.

"There were bruises on Kay Richards's face and arms," Shawn's father said after a few moments. "Do you have any idea how she got them? Did you observe any kind of struggle?"

"No," I answered, staring out the window at the soft rain. "I did not."

Afterward my father met us in the outer office, and we drove back from the police station. When we got home, I went upstairs to my room. It was still raining, and the house was full of the sound of it. They hadn't asked me about what I had done with Kay on the bank of the river the day before, but I would be asked about it later, and my answers would figure into the prosecutor's description of her.

Downstairs, my parents argued. "Were you talking with her?"

I heard my father say. "I don't want you talking with either of them."

"Did you expect me to tell her she couldn't come in?" my mother asked him. "They're good friends, Kevin. What do you want me to tell them?"

"The truth. That David's death is being investigated and we can't see them right now."

"Or should I tell them that the only way you can find to live with this is to blame someone?"

"You're managing to live with it, aren't you?" my father said.

"I'm grieving as much as you are."

I heard the door open then and the sound of the rain, minutes later the truck driving away again. When I went downstairs, my mother was still crying. "What did you tell them at the police station?" she asked me.

I walked over to the refrigerator and took out a pitcher of tea and drank from it. There was a large envelope on the counter from the coach at Bard College, addressed to me. "I answered their questions," I told her.

"Michael, did Kay push your brother off the bridge?"

"I don't know."

"It makes no sense that she would push him. None of it makes any sense."

I turned away and started walking back to the hallway.

"Michael." She came up behind me, and then I started crying. "You don't have to remember it right now," she said. And for a long time she held me in the middle of the kitchen, as if I were a little kid.

Kay

———

M Y   M O T H E R   W O U L D   spend hours lost with
her clay. When I was little, I used to sit in the barn
she had turned into a studio and listen to her pound it against
the wooden workbench or watch her work it with her hands,
making clay masks and sculptures of all sizes with elaborate
armatures. She liked working with the clay from the river. Her
skin would be gray from it, and the dust covered her clothing.
Sometimes she spent all night working, and when I came out in
the morning looking for her, I would find her either asleep with
her head on the bench or still working away at some piece.

"Oh, is it morning?" she would ask, looking at me, dazed.
"Let's have a look."

And then she would scoop me up in her arms and carry me
out into the yard or through the field or down to the river to see
the sun that had come up. Much of what she made was never
finished, but piled on the shelves and in the corners of the barn.
The ones she did end up finishing were strange and spectacular,
like some new species. You could see the human body in them,

but also something darker and freer. She would take the shape of a face and warp it with subtle curves or unravel the tendons of a leg, as if the forms were breaking out of themselves.

When I was little, I liked the playful ones, the mask with turquoise eye shadow and a bright red mouth or the hand that grew out of a leg and was playing an instrument. But now I like the more chaotic pieces, the ones with suggestions of so many movements they make any emotion possible.

The only things she ever gave herself to totally were me and her art. At first, with a new boyfriend or lover, she would be excited, but about the time I got to know them and we fell into a comfortable routine of shared dinners and overnights, she would end it. "I need more time for my work" was her usual excuse. Or "Kay needs more of me."

Jen was her only close friend. At school, in the art department, she had colleagues who respected her work but were jealous of her success. Jen would stay up at night with her, talking while she worked or helping to prepare the clay. Sometimes she would just watch. Jen was the type of person who brought over freshly baked bread or carried a pot of tea to the barn. They planted flowers in the spring and summer, large perennial beds, digging and separating, watering and feeding. Sometimes my mother's students came out to visit her. They were usually young men in awe of her. But most of the time, if it weren't for Jen and me, my mother would have worked and lived alone.

Once I got older, I realized there were rumors about my mother. She had been so in love with the man who was my father that she could never be happy with anyone else. She had a sexual desire that couldn't be satisfied for long by one lover. She was gay. I think the truth is that her life has always been her art.

Before we moved to the valley, I went everywhere with her, playing on the floor while she worked, sitting with her in classes and riding to the store in a backpack or on a seat strapped to her bicycle, her sidekick. At first she hated leaving me with Jen.

"I worry about you all day," she'd complain. "Every now and then I still look for you in the room," she'd tell me.

Sometimes now, when I look back, I think Jen and my mother loved one another. It was the kind of love that came of transplanting flowers into each other's gardens every summer and Jen's staying up brewing coffee all night while my mother worked. And from telling stories and laughter. From taking care of the animals Jen saved.

I can see Jen now with a chipmunk in the pocket of her sweater or stroking a baby fox. When they were healed, she drove them up into the woods and let them go. Maybe she thought of my mother as something that needed caring for. Or maybe something in Jen was drawn to my mother's rampages of creativity. They would last a week or more at a time, and when they were over, she would sleep off and on for a few days in a row, sometimes sleeping straight through the classes she was supposed to be teaching. Jen would bring over dinner for us or send the boys to get me. I spent so much time in their house that she was like a second mother for me, feeding me, brushing out my hair, telling me to wash my hands or clean up. She taught the three of us about the animals she took care of, enlisting our help to cut tape or gauze or to put on gloves and help to hold them.

"Why do you do this?" I remember asking her about the animals once when I got older.

"I don't know, Kay," she said after thinking about it. "Maybe it's like with your mother and her sculptures."

The day after the memorial service the police officer who had questioned me came to our house again. Earlier that morning I had walked over to David and Michael's. My mother had gone up to the university, and it was raining. I stood for a while in their yard with the water going through me. Then I went to their door.

Jen let me inside. The house was dark and filled with the sound of the rain. I took off the poncho I was wearing and stood by the door dripping. Michael and his dad were out. Jen asked if I was okay. She took the poncho from me and hung it up.

"Come in and dry off," she said gently. "Would you like some tea?"

"All right," I told her.

She went over to the sink and filled the kettle, putting it on the stove, then got a cup down from the cabinet and took out the box of tea bags. "I've been going through his books," she said a few minutes later as she poured the hot water.

I took the cup she offered and followed her into their family room, where there were books piled on the table and floor. I remember noticing the odd familiarity of the sofa and the rocker. "He used to jot notes to himself in the margins. I hated it, like he was ruining the books." She sat down on the floor next to a pile and picked up a couple of history volumes and a book on Eastern religion. I had started shivering. "There's notes in these and in that stack of novels on the

table. Some of the books, like the history volumes, I didn't
know he'd read."

She put the books down and picked up a paperback copy of
The Tempest. "He took notes in all of these," she said, gesturing
to the stack of plays by Shakespeare.

I sat down on the floor and picked up the volume of *Hamlet.*
Everything felt wet—my clothing and the rug I sat on, even the
pages I touched.

"He even wrote on the pages of this Doonesbury book," she
said. "He usually wrote in pencil. That was his concession to my
concerns about him ruining the books."

I watched while she looked through more of them. "Someone brought me a possum last night," she said. "It was found on
the road with its babies. It's in a cage out back. I almost got bit
trying to get it in there."

"I don't know how it happened," I told her.

She got up and carried my emptied cup to her kitchen. "You
should go before Kevin and Michael get home," she said when
she came back.

I put on the wet poncho, and then she gave me one of the
Shakespeare volumes, putting her arms around my shoulders and
holding me for a moment before opening the door. I stepped
outside and stood under the overhang, watching the sheets of
rain. Before I walked back, I stuck the book inside my clothes
and saw it was the copy of *Hamlet.*

———

THAT AFTERNOON WHEN I was questioned, Officer Townsend requested that I come with him to the police station in town. It would be necessary, he said, for them to get my permission to tape-record my answers. My mother was still away teaching her classes, and there were written instructions from her lying on the kitchen table telling me to eat lunch, then drive over to the campus. I was to meet her at her office, and she would go with me to the dean's office, where I had an appointment to discuss what allowances they would make for my taking incompletes for the spring semester.

It was ten o'clock and I had just gotten dressed. I was finding my mother's managing of my life a relief as I went numbly through the actions.

"I'm supposed to meet my mother at the university," I told the officer. Behind him I could see a woman officer sitting in the patrol car.

"I'll wait while you call her," he said. "Tell her she can meet us there if she wants to."

My mother wasn't in her studio, so I left a message on her machine and went outside and got into the patrol car. The short trip in the back of the police car was eerie, my reflection on the window transposed onto the dark fields and trees along the roadside. The police station was in the small business area just across from the town hall and the library. I recognized someone I saw working there as the parent of a girl I had gone to school with. Officer Townsend and the woman who was with us in the car took me to a small room in the back of the station. From the window I could see the coffee shop where David, Michael, and I had hung out while we were in high school.

The young woman officer had a quiet manner. She read me my rights, stating that I could have a lawyer if I wanted one, but I wasn't sure who that would be, and I told myself that the fastest way to get through this was to answer their questions.

They went through most of the same questions I had answered the week before, but more slowly and methodically, asking me where the acid had come from, if I had known of any prior drug use, and how long David and I had known each other.

Then the woman officer flipped through the pages of a notebook in front of her. "How were you and David getting along recently?" she asked me, glancing up from the pages.

"What do you mean?"

She turned another page, and I saw her eyes sweep across it. "Had you had any disagreements or differences of opinion?"

"I'm not sure why you're asking that," I said, staring at the notebook. "Sometimes we would disagree about what to do or where to meet or something."

She looked up coolly, as if she were considering me as our eyes met. "Did he have any other girlfriends that you knew of?"

"No."

"Were you seeing anyone else?"

"No," I answered, pausing, staring at the page from the notebook that was suspended in her hand. "I wasn't."

"Was jealousy ever a problem? Was it ever something you talked about or fought over?"

I looked down at the table. Recently David had spent several evenings working with someone on a project for a class. Another time he had gone out with a group of people, including someone I thought he liked. Sometimes I would see him in the dining hall sitting and talking with a girl from one of his classes. "No," I heard my answer.

"You're sure?" she said, giving the notebook a little push so that it rested on the table between us. "Take a minute to think about it."

No one said anything for a few minutes. Officer Townsend leaned over and picked up the notebook himself, glancing at it. "Would you like a Coke or something else to drink?" he asked me.

I said that I would have a Coke, and he went out of the room for a minute. I thought about how David had put his arms around me before he got onto the rail, how he had slid his hands inside my pants and that was the last thing I had had of him. Then Officer Townsend came back with a Coke can and plastic cup. I watched him pour some of it into the glass.

"What about the jealousy?" the woman asked when he had handed it to me and I had sipped a little of it.

"I might have been jealous once in a while," I said, feeling the Coke bubble back up into my nose. "But he didn't have any other girlfriends."

"You were jealous of other girls?"

No, I thought. I was picturing a girl he had dated the year before. I'd wanted to know everything he'd done with her, but he hadn't told me. "You need to have more friends," my mother used to tell me, but there wasn't room for them. "Sometimes," I answered now.

She leaned toward me. "Did you ever say anything to him about feeling that way?"

I looked at her and thought how this was mine and I didn't

want her to have any of it. Then I told her that he'd had a girl-friend the year before at college, when I was still in high school. I said I'd asked about her.

"And when you did, what happened?"

"I don't really remember," I told her. "I think he laughed about it or made a joke."

"So he wouldn't tell you about this girlfriend?"

"No." The notebook was on the table again, and she touched the spiral end that lay between the pages. I watched her run her finger along it.

"Was there an argument about her?"

Sometimes I cried, I thought. Sometimes I fell apart, like I couldn't hold all of it. "I don't remember."

"But there was some jealousy?" she asked.

I nodded slightly, looking down at myself.

"Could you say yes so that the tape recorder picks it up?"

"Yes," I answered, dropping my face into my hands.

It was quiet for a moment then, and I could hear the pages of the notebook being turned. Then I heard her slide it across the table. "We have on record that you each swallowed one tablet of LSD at five-thirty P.M. on the night in question. Is that correct?"

"Yes."

"Then about eleven P.M., the three of you went out for a drive in David's car."

I nodded. "Yes."

"David was driving?" I glanced up at her, and she tried again to hold my gaze, but I wasn't seeing anything I looked at.

"Yes."

She took the notebook back from Officer Townsend. "Why didn't Michael drive?"

"David's driving didn't seem to be a problem," I said slowly.

"What do you mean, his driving didn't seem to be a problem?"

"He wasn't speeding. He was staying in the right lane."

She looked at me for a full minute. "You didn't perceive any danger?"

"No." I stared at the table. I could hear the woman officer saying something to Officer Townsend.

"First you drove out to the railroad crossing by Routes Five and Ten," she said, turning back to me. "Where did David stop the car?"

I thought about that drive before we reached the bridge and how David kept saying, "I'm one hundred and fifty percent operable." I was looking out the window watching the way the road unwound.

"Where did David stop the car?" she asked again.

"On the tracks," I told her.

"Why would he do something like that?"

"He moved it before the train came," I said, thinking that the roar of the train had filled the car but that he had moved it and that this was what mattered.

"All right." She looked over at Townsend. He had turned around, and I saw that he was pressing a button on the recorder. "So what happened after you stopped the car on the train tracks?"

"Michael got out."

She raised her eyebrows slightly. "And you stayed in the car with David?"

"Yes."

"Did you say anything to him while you were sitting there, before the train came?"

There had been the pounding of the wheels on the track, the screech of the whistle, then the blinding light, and we felt the push from the speed of the train as the car slid off onto the gravel. "Not that I can remember," I told her. "I think he said that he was moving the car."

"How did it feel," she asked, "when you were sitting in the car like that? Was it boring or fun or frightening? Was it exciting?"

"I don't know," I told her.

"Why didn't you try to convince him to move the car? You could have been killed sitting like that on the tracks."

I thought about the speed of the train and how we had been close enough to the tracks that I'd felt the rush of air push us across the gravel. "I don't remember."

"You don't remember." She paused. "What happened next? Do you remember that?"

I looked at her. She had pushed the notebook to the side so that only the table was between us now. She had her arms on it and was leaning toward me, her head turned to one side, the way you turn it when you're trying to hear something that is far away. "We tried to make Michael get back into the car. He was walking on the road, and we drove up alongside him, and he and David argued. Michael said he was walking home, but that was more than five miles away, and we kept telling him it was too far, until he finally got back in."

It was quiet then, and after a few minutes the woman officer got up and went over to the recorder, taking the tape out and checking it and putting it back in. Officer Townsend cleared his throat. He picked up a pencil and tapped it slightly on the table. "What happened when you got to the bridge?" he asked me. "Was there more arguing?"

I thought for a minute. David stopping the car, how I had almost not opened the door. "We might still be tripping," I'd said to him. Then the kiss, the three of us climbing out of the car. "Michael didn't want to walk across," I said now. "He tried to get us to go back off the bridge with him."

"Was there an argument over it?"

"Yes," I answered.

The woman officer sat down again and looked at the notebook, turning a page in it. "When we questioned you last week, you stated that there was no argument," she told me. "Were you trying to protect yourself?"

There was a long silence. I could feel the chair beneath me, how it supported me. I could hear the slight hum of an overhead light and the running of the cassette in the recorder. Had there been an argument? Now I wasn't sure.

"What happened next?" Townsend asked finally.

"Michael went back by himself and got into the car, and David looked out across the river."

The woman officer glanced at Townsend. "Did you have any physical contact while you were standing there?" she asked me.

Yes, I thought, of course. "We were standing close together," I told her.

"Did you embrace at all? Did you kiss one another?"

I wondered where he was suddenly, and it felt oddly as if he could be in the room with us, listening, amused. "Yes," I answered, unable to remember what I had answered the first time.

"How did you sustain the bruises on your face and arm?"

"I don't know."

She leaned nearer, the blue shirt of her uniform pressing against the table. "Think about it."

"I can't remember."

"You were standing very close together. There was a lot of arguing in the car and on the bridge. Did you argue while you were standing there close together?"

"No."

"What did you talk about?"

I thought about how we had stood together on the bridge and how it was the last time, and it made me angry that she would ask me about it. "He said things about the river and about jumping from the rail."

"What kinds of things?"

"About the sound the water was making. He said we should jump in and swim to the shore. He said we could make it."

"What did you say?" the woman asked.

"I don't remember."

It was quiet for a moment again, both officers watching me. I thought about how his mouth had felt when it was over my mouth and how it had seemed to go on a long time when we were standing there. "I think you do remember," the woman officer said finally.

I shrugged. He had put his hands inside my clothes, then turned toward the rail. Like an orgasm, I had thought. As if the jump would be the sex. "I didn't say very much. I told him I would."

"Your boyfriend asks you to jump off a bridge over one hundred feet into the river, and you didn't say very much back to him except that you would do it?" She paused, drumming her fingers against the table.

"What happened next?" Townsend asked.

"He climbed up on the railing," I told them.

"Did you help him?"

I looked at Townsend, then at the woman officer. I thought about the fact that this was none of their business and that what was there between David and me wasn't there for anyone else. "Yes," I said finally.

"You helped him to climb onto the railing?"

"I was holding on to him, steadying him."

"Did you hold on to him as he stood up?" the woman officer asked.

I closed my eyes. I had held on to him the entire time, as if that could have kept us together. "I had my hands on his legs."

"What happened next?" She slid her arm across the table as if she meant to touch me.

"He jumped off," I said quietly.

"He jumped?" Townsend asked. "He didn't fall?"

I looked over at him for a moment. His face was insistent but puzzled. You can't have a clue, I thought. "Yes. He jumped."

"Did you understand that it was dangerous, even though you were high?" he asked me.

I saw the water, how far it was underneath the bridge, and the outline of his body against the sky. "Yes," I answered. "I knew."

"Where were your hands when he was standing on the rail?" the woman officer asked suddenly.

"They were on his legs," I said.

"Why?"

"I don't know. I was just helping him."

"Helping him to jump?"

I looked down at myself. I was wearing the gray university sweatshirt that two weeks ago David had lent me. I remembered how he had picked it up off the chair in his room and handed it to me the last night I spent there. "For you," he had said, bowing elaborately. I had pulled it over my head before I went to his house this morning, and it smelled still vaguely of him.

"No," I told the officers. "I wouldn't have done that. I was just helping him to stand on the rail."

"I think you're lying. You pushed him, didn't you?"

"No, I didn't. I really don't think I did."

"You don't *think* you did? Are you certain about what happened? There's a lot about that night that you've admitted you don't remember."

She looked at me for a full minute, and I thought how strange it was, my being there and the intensity of her expression and how her face would be in my head the rest of my life. "No."

"No, what?"

"No, I'm not certain."

Officer Townsend wrote something in the notebook. He held the pen up while he addressed me. "Kay, where were your hands?"

"They were around his knees I think," I said, trying not to cry. "I really don't remember, but I know I didn't push him."

For a minute no one said anything. The tape reached its end, and as I heard the cassette being ejected, I felt an enormous relief to have it over with.

"There are pieces of your story that don't add up," the woman officer addressed me as Officer Townsend switched off the tape player. "Do you know what perjury means?"

I nodded.

"It's a serious offense."

There was a knock on the door then. "Kay Richards's mother is here. She wants to come back," another officer told them.

"Tell her we're done," Townsend said.

The woman officer watched me as I stood up. "Think about what I said," she told me.

We walked down the short hallway then to the main desk at the entrance as my mother came toward us. She had on the clay-covered denim overalls she wore when she worked, and her hair was tied back in a scarf. "You brought her in without notifying me," she said accusingly.

"She's over eighteen," Townsend replied. "She decided not to call a lawyer or to wait until you could be reached."

My mother took my arm, pulling me to her. "Were you interrogating her?" she asked.

Townsend shrugged. The woman officer I noticed had gone back down the hall and into the room we'd been in. "She's free to go," Townsend said. "There's no charge."

My mother pushed me toward the door. I let my eyes meet Townsend's for a moment. I was wondering what they were going to do with the tape. "I'm going to find out if this is legal," my mother told him.

BY THE NEXT morning, my mother had a consultation arranged with a lawyer. Mr. West, the brother of one of my mother's friends, was middle-aged and bald, the kind of lawyer who handled messy divorce settlements. Before the year was out, she would hire a succession of three different lawyers and spend most of what she'd saved for my college education and her own retirement.

The lawyer's office was near the university, in an old house that had been turned into several suites. Mr. West was on the first floor, where a parlor had probably once been, with a closed-off fireplace, a conference-size table, and several large chairs. When we sat down in them that morning, he told us that he hadn't talked with the police yet or gotten a look at the transcript from the interview they'd held with me, but that he'd gathered from what he had found out that this was a drug investigation, typical of those that followed any drug-related death.

"Beyond determining cause, there's pressure put on them to figure out where the drug came from," he explained. "They'll probably want to know how much you took and who supplied it. They might be hoping to get an arrest."

"An arrest?" my mother asked, sliding her chair in close under the table. She was wearing a colorful plaid skirt, and she had one of the bright scarves she often wore draped around her neck. A pair of long earrings that looked like pieces of silver lace swung next to her face whenever she moved.

The lawyer stared at me for a second, in my sweatshirt and jeans, and then back at my mother. "Of the person who sold him the acid."

"So why did they take Kay to the station to question her a second time? I was there the first time when they came to the house. It seemed like they asked everything they should have needed to then. Kay doesn't know where he got the acid."

Mr. West shrugged. "I can't say for sure, but it's not unusual to bring someone in for a second interview."

"They read her her rights."

There was a piece of paper on the table, and Mr. West wrote something on it. "It's usually a precaution. They like to protect themselves in case anything is said that they later need to use as evidence. From what you've told me, it sounds like they wanted her statement on tape."

My mother turned and looked at me for a moment. I thought of the time when she'd gone in and talked to the principal of the high school after I'd done badly in a few of my classes. "They asked Kay a lot of questions about her relationship with David," she told Mr. West. "And they wanted details about what happened that night after they went out for the drive."

"What kinds of questions?" he asked.

I looked at the fireplace. An arrangement of dried flowers was placed in front of it, thistle and amaranth, plants my mother had grown. I closed my eyes for a second, touching the edge of the chair underneath me. "They wanted to know how we got along and if we fought at all. And they asked questions about what had happened that night."

"What did you tell them?"

"I told them how we walked out onto the bridge and what David had said while we were standing by the railing, that he wanted to jump off the bridge and that he could swim to the side. He got up on the railing after that."

"Were the three of you on the bridge together?"

"No. Michael had gone back to the car. It was just the two of us." I watched him make a note of this.

"Did you help him get onto the railing?"

I glanced from Mr. West to my mother. There were lines that had formed on her face recently, and I thought how she would be old soon, an aging hippie. "Did you help him?" West repeated.

"He steadied himself by holding on to my shoulders. I supported him while he was on it."

"However, it was his idea, and he initiated the act?" He tapped his pen on the table, marking the distinction.

I nodded.

My mother brushed her scarf away from her neck and pulled at the long necklace she had on. "What are you getting at?" she asked him.

"There's not a Good Samaritan law in this state. That would mean that you could be held accountable for not talking someone out of committing suicide or stopping a dangerous act if you had the ability to stop it."

We both sat there for a moment taking this in. I was feeling oddly disconnected, as if whatever was said about that night really didn't matter anymore. "Do you think she could be held responsible for what happened?" my mother asked him.

Mr. West shook his head. "That's doubtful. This is probably a drug investigation. They need to establish Kay's relationship with David and find out how he was acting before he jumped off the bridge. The state attorney's office will have to decide on whether to rule the death as accidental or suicide."

I gripped the chair suddenly and bent forward, the taste of vomit in the back of my throat. "Do you need some water?" Mr. West got up and disappeared for a moment. My mother leaned over me, and I felt her hand slide across my back.

"Are you all right?" She handed me the cup of water that Mr. West brought back with him, and when I drank from it, the water sprayed out onto her skirt. I slumped forward and sat like that for a while, with my head on my knees, shivering. My mother rested her hand on my back, and for the first time in several years that I could remember, I wanted it there.

"You should probably take her home," Mr. West told her. "I'll read through the police transcript and give you a call. What I would recommend at this point is making sure she doesn't talk with the police again without me present. Chances are they won't contact her again, but if they do, call my office. If I can't get down there, I have an assistant who is very good, and she'll be there. Meanwhile, I would find a psychologist for Kay to talk to. Get something on record about her psychological state since the incident."

He paused for a moment, and I heard my mother pick up the bag she had carried in with her. "How well do you know the Sandersons?" Mr. West asked her suddenly.

"We've been good friends—best friends, really—for years, since we moved here. Why?"

"Have you talked to them since the incident?"

"Of course." She settled slowly back into her chair, her hand on my hair, twisting it into a loose knot that fell down my back. "Right afterward I went over there quite a bit. I took food, and I helped Jen plan the memorial service. I've been dating a friend of theirs, and he was over there also."

Mr. West wrote again on the paper. "The service was when?" he asked, his pen lifted.

"Two days ago, this past weekend."

"Have you talked since then?"

She paused for a minute. "Once, on the phone. It was brief. I was going to call tonight."

"What about the man you're dating?"

"We've both been wrapped up in this. We haven't had a chance to talk about it much."

Mr. West nodded. He gazed at the paper, thinking.

My mother pulled two of the rings off her fingers and put them back on. It was a habit of hers, which had driven me crazy when I was younger. "Why do you want to know?"

"Sometimes the family will push to have something like this investigated. That's probably unlikely in this case. Most people would want it over with quickly, given the fact that drugs were involved and that there's already been an article in the paper. Plus, their other son was present." He stood up, then leaned over the table and wrote something else on the sheet of paper. "Are you back in school?" he asked me.

I got up, closing my eyes again, trying to push back the nausea. "She's getting incompletes in most of her classes," my mother told him.

He wrote something else on the pad in front of him. "Get the psychologist's evaluation," he said as he stepped around his desk and shook my mother's hand. "With any luck we won't even need to talk again."

I threw up once we were in the parking lot. "He didn't commit suicide," my mother said when we finally got into the car. "You know that. It was accidental. He was high, and his judgment was distorted. So was yours. I'm just grateful you didn't jump with him."

I didn't say anything back. When we got home, I lay down while my mother went out to empty her kiln at the university and run a couple of errands. Later she came back with the local newspaper, which had an editorial in it claiming that the problems with drugs at the university were the result of faculty and parents who did not take the situation seriously. The author referred to David's death as an example.

"Jen and Kevin will be upset by this," she said as she picked up the phone and dialed their number. When no one answered, I listened to her leave a message. Then she called Jonathan.

I didn't hear much of their conversation, but when she got off, I could tell she'd been crying.

"What's the matter?" I asked.

"Nothing." She shrugged. "He can be distant sometimes. I guess we've all been under a lot of pressure."

Later that evening I ate some dinner with her for the first time in the week since David had died. Afterward we were sitting on the back step, drinking coffee, when Mr. West called. I remember my mother going inside to get the phone while I stayed on the step staring at the tulips that had just opened by the fence in the backyard. David was gone, I told myself, but nothing about it registered.

When my mother came back, she stood behind me for a minute resting her hands against my head. She took a long breath then and slid down next to me, and I could feel the width of her body, how it was when I was small and she would hold me against her. "Who was it?" I asked her.

"The lawyer, Mr. West. He's read through the police transcript, and he thinks we should consider a different kind of lawyer. He gave me a couple of names. He doesn't think this a drug investigation anymore. He said he wasn't sure at this point what the police are after."

Kevin

AFTER THE MEMORIAL service I still can't get myself to stop thinking about him. Late into the night I lie awake seeing things and picking the images clean—black mussels, the mosslike green sponges, and the crayfish feeding along the bottom of the river. I see his body lying among them, the denim on his legs, the hair on his head, his eyes floating in his face. I imagine the fire of the crematorium and the container they've stored the ashes in.

As the night wears on, I go downstairs and sit at my desk. He was bright and creative. I imagine him as he would have been years from now, the dreams he would have dreamed and what he would have achieved. I close my eyes and hear what Michael said when we were in the car after the service. I see the underwear that was stuffed in his pocket.

For several years now I've been working on a book about the history of the Connecticut River valley. Last fall I was paired with a geologist as part of a lecture series. During the Ice Age, a glacier covered the area, and when it melted, an enormous lake developed. Driving around, you can still see the outline where its shores were, and along the bottom of the river lie vast clay deposits and layers of sediment in symmetrical patterns like the rings on a tree. Eventually all of us become part of something large and rhythmic. The problem is in the here and now, where morality is still important. What are the causes of an event? Who can be held accountable?

The article that came out in the newspaper the day before the memorial service blamed me and Jen. Kay was unavailable for comment, and Ellen's only remark was that there was a large party at our house the night David jumped. Jen and I came off sounding like liberal parents who were too relaxed about our kid's illegal activities.

"Experimentation with drugs is something parents who grew up in the sixties and seventies, when drugs were prevalent, may find difficult to condemn," the writer stated. "When something like this happens, it's important that the community give a clear message: A death like David Sanderson's is tragic and reckless."

After that, the articles and editorials abound. Our phone rings constantly with reporters from newspapers in Springfield and Boston, and every idiot fond of empty moralizing fills up the editorial page with letters and commentary about what can go wrong with benign neglect or what happens when parents lose touch with their teenage children.

Jen stops answering the phone. She sets up counseling services for Michael and tries to convince me to go to a grief group with her. I overhear her making arrangements for starting a memorial fund in David's name. Late at night she stays up nursing a stray cat she's found. White tape and rolls of gauze litter the kitchen counter, an envelope of pills, a pair of tweezers.

All of it makes me crazy—the injured animal, the sound of her voice, the trees beginning to flesh out the banks of the river. "Michael saw her push him," I tell her. "How can you think about a grief group? How can you spend all this time working on a cat?"

Greg Townsend brings Michael in for questioning the day after the funeral, and I end up in his office the next morning, nearly knocking over the chair as I start to sit down on it. "I want to know what's going on with the investigation," I tell him.

He looks up from the paperwork that's spread across his desk. "You know I can't go into that with you," he says.

It's been over a week since I slept. I have trouble even making myself slow down long enough to do things like take showers. "I want to see what you've got," I tell him, running my hand over the rough beard that's started growing on my face.

He picks up a folder and places it at the far corner of his desk. The desk's surface is covered with pen and pencil markings, the finish on the wood nearly worn through. "Up until two days ago we were treating this as an accident," he says, grimacing. "I'm moving as fast as I can to get information, but it's been more than a week since it happened."

"What have you done so far?"

"After we questioned Michael, we brought Kay Richards in for a lengthy interview. I'm still putting everything together. I've notified the district attorney's office that we may have something, and I'll give it to them as soon as I can."

I lean over, lowering the weight of my head into my hands. Greg is from this area. His roots go back several generations, and even though our paths have crossed often because of Michael and his son Shawn, I'm guessing he still sees us as newcomers. "This is sorry-assed," I tell him, my palms digging into my forehead. "You gave up searching the river for him after a few days. Now, when it's obvious he was pushed, you're stalling on an arrest. You're writing him off."

I lower my hands to glance up at him. He shakes his head. "No," he starts to say. Then someone opens his door and sticks her head in. "Give me a minute, will you?" he tells her. "I am *not* writing him off," he says when the door is closed. "I didn't expect this thing to change directions the way it has. I can't get an arrest without enough evidence. If we act too quickly, we'll end up jeopardizing the case."

He pauses for a moment, and I look up again to see him signaling someone else who has put a head in his doorway to back out and shut it again. "Have you been keeping up with the articles in the newspapers?" I ask him.

He lets out a deep breath. "Reporters can be stupid. The ones who write editorials are usually worse. You have to ignore anything the media says."

I raise my arm too fast, trying to object, and my hand hits the side of his desk. "How the hell am I supposed to do that?"

"Kevin, stop," he says leaning toward me, his hand on my arm. I feel the firmness of it, the width of his fingers. "Number one, obviously you need to start getting some sleep. And number two, are you teaching again yet?"

"I'm taking at least another week," I tell him, lowering my

head again, staring at a spot on the floor. "There are a couple of different people covering my classes."

"Good," he says. "That's good. Call your doctor. See a therapist or something. Take some time to sort out your emotions."

I hunch myself in closer to the desk and lower my voice. "I don't need to sort out my emotions. What I need is to know what happened to my son."

"I told you, I'm working on that," he says, waiting for me to raise my head again, then looking at me closely. "I'm doing little else but working on that." He picks up a pen and starts tapping it against his desk. "Have you come across any of David's journals or notebooks since this happened, something that might have been in his bedroom or dorm room that he was writing in?"

I think about the articles that have been in the paper, the stance they've all taken that he was drug user. The tapping of the pen gets on my nerves. "Why? What do you want them for?"

"There may be references in them that we can use," he says, letting the pen drop now, almost purposefully, again and again.

"References to drugs?"

"Maybe. And references to Kay." He sets the pen down on the desk, then picks it up, writing something on a small pad of paper. "Actually, we'd like to get the family's permission to go through his dorm room."

I stare at him for a moment. I'm aware of how dry and blood-shot my eyes feel, of the stubble that's on my face. It occurs to me that since this happened, I haven't even been inside David's dorm room. "Would that be all right?" he asks.

"I should check with Jen first."

He says something else about the sleep I need to be getting and if I've talked with a doctor. He asks about Jen. Then I stand up slowly, and as my legs and back unfold, I have the feeling that I could be falling instead, as if my equilibrium is seriously upset. He walks me through the outer office, holding the door to the station open for me. I feel his hand on my arm. "Take care of yourself," he says. Then he stands there watching while I get into the truck and pull out.

At first I don't pay attention to the road, my mind turning everything over, but suddenly, as I round a bend near the river, I see it all clearly—the dark, muddy fields and the upper branches of the trees feathered toward the sky. Part of my brain is split off, making connections. There's the moral imperative, the historical perspective. Of course, psychological explanations abound. An imperative, for example, is easier than grief. I glance at the birches along the river, their silver silhouettes. He would be sitting next to me in the cab of the truck, seeing what I am seeing, or else he'd up at the university right now writing a paper or beginning to study for exams. As I pull over next to a gravel road that goes down to the river, images are recurring again, unbidden—the clouds of silt, tiny particles of it floating near the bottom, layers of sediment, the shoe tumbling through the water. Impossible, the split-off part is commenting. You spent six days walking the bank, and it was impossible.

I don't go home first or even try to contact Jen. This is about somehow saving what's left of us. It's about David and when he was little and I'd carry him on my back through the woods and Jen would be walking in front of us with her light brown hair all long and streaks of red in it from the sun. On fire, I used to say. Gleaming.

I turn around, pulling back onto the road, and thirty minutes later I'm walking down the hallway of the dorm where his suite was, trying to find a resident assistant or one of the kids who lived with him to give me a key. Spring break has ended, and the dorm is active with kids coming and going carrying their backpacks, talking and laughing with one another. Eventually Joel comes by, a kid David was friends with since freshman year, and he lets me into the suite, then digs around until he finds the extra key they had to David's room.

"We didn't know what to do with it," he says as I unlock the door to David's bedroom. "They told us you would come and get his things. None of us has been in there."

I haven't seen the room since the fall, shortly after David moved in, and when I open the door, the first thing I notice is how typical it is—the requisite books and papers on the desk, a few items of dirty laundry thrown across a chair, a poster advertising a campus movie on one of the walls, his guitar propped against the closet door. It gets to me, how ordinary it is, like so many other rooms on this campus you could walk into, and for a moment, as I hear Joel shutting the door behind me, my breath is taken away.

Maybe what I expected was something more specific and personal, or the sense that David could still be somewhere inside, as if the air might peel away, pregnant with him.

I move around the room, touching things haphazardly—a textbook that's on his desk, a pen he's recently held, a battered

Frisbee, a rock flecked with mica fragments. There's a smudge of
ink on the desk's surface, the glitter of the mica. He had started
writing a paper or a short story, and I find what looks like an
unfinished lab report and a page of notes on Shakespeare:
" 'Who are we?' is the central question of the plays."

Eventually I start going through his desk drawers, hoping to
find a private notebook or journal. There are the usual things—
calculators, rulers, a bottle of glue, colored pencils, and rolls of
tape. Then from the back of the last drawer I pull out a plastic
case like the kind you would keep pencils in and open the lid.
Inside, with paper clips and an ink pen, is a plastic envelope with
a zipper, which I pull, and inside that is a small plastic bag of
what looks like marijuana. Wrapped in notebook paper next to
it are at least a dozen small blue tablets.

At first, the reality of it makes no sense, and then the betrayal
sinks in, but instead of feeling angry, I feel disconnected, so that
the *room* doesn't make sense anymore. The pile of books and the
paper on his desk spread out like a kind of collage. I pick up a
sheet that he's written on and see the mesh of fiber and the throb
of black ink. There's also a kind of fear, the worn Converse
sneaker on the floor next to my foot like a shoe for the dead.

I pick up the case again, and as I start to slip the drugs back
into it, I see the photographs in the bottom, black-and-white
pictures that look like they were taken with the Polaroid we
bought a year or so ago. All of them are of Kay. In one of them
her shirt is pulled down to show most of her breasts, and the
expression on her face is provocative. David is in several of the
photographs with her. They're kissing, and she's not wearing
the shirt anymore. In some of them she is turned around to face

him on his lap, her legs straddling him with her skirt lifted—
they could be having sex. Her breasts are larger than I would
have thought, pendulous. In one of the frames she holds them
outward, cupped in her hands, the nipples hardened.

I set the photos carefully on his desk, then slide the drugs
back into the pencil case again, placing it in the briefcase I've
brought with me. I think of the water eating away his flesh, of
her hips riding against his. Ellen is known for a group of sculptures that look like bodies, just inhuman enough to put you on
edge. Several years ago, when she started helping Jen with
wildlife rehabilitation, the animal forms crept into them, as if she
was saying that we all are on the verge of animalness, just by
being human. "Thousands of years of civilization have undone
that," I remember arguing with her. "That's what history is
about."

When Kay was younger, I wondered why Ellen didn't find
someone to settle down with. Kay would spend all day running
through the fields or in the woods, so that her clothes were
always dirty and torn and her hair got so matted that everyone
gave up brushing it and Jen just cut it back every few months.
Kay had the kind of undisciplined nature that did not adapt well
to school, so that she would do well on one lesson but fail
another that didn't hold her interest. Then she turned into a
teenager who was both highly emotional and voluptuous. I was
relieved the year David went off to college and Michael got
involved enough in basketball that he spent less time with her.

I leave the photographs on his desk and quickly go through
the rest of the drawers and closet, finding several notebooks
from the classes he was taking and one bound journal, all of

which I place in the briefcase. The room still feels out of place, nonsensical. I try to picture him in it, wearing the denim hat or lining up the glass bottles from soft drinks and beer on the windowsill, but I have no idea when he acquired so many of the objects, as if there is no timeline anymore, only one tense.

Maybe the images I have of him were simply outdated. I can picture him at eight, all curiosity and quickness, or at fourteen, skinny after a growth spurt, a kind of awkward grace. He grew up too fast, I tell myself. Eight, then ten, suddenly nineteen and involved with Kay in something I'll never understand.

Then as I'm leaving, I happen to pick up the pair of worn jeans draped over the chair. I hold them up in front of me, and the folds and creases in the denim still hold the shape of his body.

I'm numb as I get into the truck and drive away. In the stairwell on my way out of the building, I ran into several of David's friends, laughing and horsing around. "It was a good service, Dr. Sanderson," they told me, standing there, suddenly awkward and strange. Now the road passes swiftly under the truck, and soon I am driving through the country, past the small farms with their newly plowed fields. I picture the way David was holding Kay. She shrugs off her shirt and undoes the fly on his pants. She slides her hands under his buttocks, her nipples brushing against him. He doesn't even take his clothes off all the way before she has him inside her, riding him as if she is being lifted into the air.

When I get home, Jen's intuition is uncanny. She comes into my study as I'm emptying the briefcase. "What is that?" she asks me.

"A couple of David's notebooks that I found." I pick one of them up, showing her.

"You were in his dorm room?" She looks at me curiously, then takes the journal and pages through it.

"I wanted to look around. We'll need to empty it out soon."

"What's this?" She picks up the case that's still in the brief-case, and before I can prevent her, she opens it. "Was this in his room?" she asks, taking out the plastic bag and opening it. She lifts it to her face then and smells. After setting it down on the desk, she unfolds the notebook paper and stands there looking at the tablets.

"What are you going to do with them?" she asks.

I reach over her and refold the paper, putting it and the plastic bag of marijuana back in the case.

She lowers her hand to the desk, resting it there next to the case. "Kevin, tell me you're planning to give that to Greg Townsend."

I put my hand on hers, noting the coolness of her fingers for a second before she slides hers out from under mine, moving away. "What would be the point in giving them to Greg now?" I ask her. "The newspapers already have David made out to be a drug user. And there is absolutely no way to know how this got into his room. Anyone could have put it there."

She glances down at the drawer, then she looks back up at me as if she means to put her hand there again. "You need to give it to Greg and let him make that decision."

"If we give it to Greg, it will confirm what the newspapers have said," I tell her.

"Greg Townsend is not the type to jump to conclusions, but the fact that they were in David's room suggests that last week was not the first time that he had used something."

Jen is not beautiful, but she's always been attractive in an elegant kind of way, with thin, smooth lines, the bones of her pelvis visible under her skin, and the sharp features. The name Jennifer or Jenny never fit her. For years I put her on a pedestal.

Before we were married, we went Canada and lived in the wilderness for two years in a rough cabin that I built beside a lake. Each morning we would fish, and we lived off what we caught and the food we grew during the summer. I pictured us staying on the lake forever, uncorrupted by anything else, a kind of Adam and Eve. Then she got pregnant with David, and we came back to the States and got married.

One day, about a year ago, when I was looking for her, I found her with Ellen in the shed behind our house, where she sometimes keeps the cage for an animal she's found. They were standing in the darkened corner, entwined with each other like a kind of puzzle, so that I couldn't tell what they were doing. Ellen laughed, and when Jen put her hands on Ellen's face, Ellen bent forward and kissed her. I dismissed it at the time as unimportant, but now, as I look at her, the image of them together mixes with those from the photographs. I remember the one where Kay's shirt had slipped off her shoulder and her hair fell down the white skin of her back.

Now Jen still stands in front of the desk, her arms crossed over chest, brooding. "These were in it also," I tell her, taking out the photographs and handing them to her. She gasps a little, and I watch the hurt of seeing him like that play out across her face. "These are a good representation of what she had him involved in. He could have gotten the drugs from her. Have you thought about that?" I ask her. "His grades went down fall semester when he started seeing her."

"There's no way for you to know that," she says too quickly, handing the photographs back to me.

I put the pictures back and close the case, then put it in one of the desk drawers. "I'm not giving any of this to anyone right now," I tell her. "I'm waiting to see what happens first."

IT'S AFTER FIVE o'clock that afternoon when Greg Townsend drives up to the house in his patrol car and comes to the door. Michael is home from school by then, closed off upstairs in his room. I answer the door before there's a knock or the ring of a bell. "Kevin, I need to have a few words with you," he says, standing there, still dressed in his uniform, looking tired and serious.

I open the door wide and motion for him to come in. Jen is fixing dinner in the kitchen. "Kevin, could you check on Michael?" she calls out.

"In a minute," I tell her.

Greg glances down the hall, in the direction of her voice, as I lead him into the dining room. "Do you want to sit?" I ask him.

"No." He waves me away. "I sent someone up to the campus this afternoon to have David's room sectioned off; thinking we would get your permission by tomorrow to search it, something I would have done right after the incident if I thought this was going to end up becoming an investigation. That person called me a few minutes ago to let me know he talked with one of the roommates, who told him you were up there this morning."

We stand there for a moment while he waits for me to say something. Finally I shrug my shoulders. "I thought I'd go ahead and get any journals or notebooks that were there and give them to you," I tell him.

He stares at me for another moment without moving any of the muscles in his face. "We've sought your cooperation," he says. "We've been treating Michael as a cooperative witness. But what you did could be seen as an obstruction of justice."

"That room's been open for a week since this happened. Anyone could have gone in there and taken something from it or stuck something in there. Now suddenly you decide—"

"It was locked."

"His roommates had a key."

He steps back from me for a minute and leans against the table. He glances past me through the doorway into the hall, and I turn around to see Jen standing there. "Look," he says, "I'd like for you to give me anything you took from the room. I'd rather have you give it to me than have to have it subpoenaed by the court."

"Fine," I tell him, glancing at Jen. "I have no problem with that. I took a journal and a few notebooks he was using for courses. I'll go and get them."

He waits in the dining room while Jen follows me into the study. "You're going to give him the case with the drugs in it, aren't you?" she asks, shutting the door behind her as I pick up the stack of notebooks and the journal from my desk. "That's what they're looking for," she adds when I don't answer her.

I tuck the journals and notebooks under my arm. "They don't know what they're looking for. If we give them the case, they'll be out here going through his stuff for weeks. If they find nothing, they'll leave us alone."

She turns, staring at the closed door. All I can see is the side and the back of her head. "I don't know if I can live with not giving it to him," she says.

"I don't know if I can live with it if you do," I say evenly.

She turns back to me. I've seen her this way before, indignant over a cause. Her eyes are almost gray in the dim light of the room, and when she talks, there's a hole inside her voice I could fall into. "It's the right thing to do. You can't withhold evidence."

"Think about what will come afterward if we show it to them. There'll be more articles in the paper, and they'll make all kinds of assumptions. Anyone could have gone into that room during the past week. There's no telling how the drugs got into his drawer, but you know what it will turn into if they're found—concrete evidence that he supplied the acid."

"I don't agree with what you're doing," she says, then stands there for a moment looking at me, her lips pressed together, before she turns her head and swings open the door to the study.

Seconds later, when I hear her walking toward the kitchen, I take the notebooks and the journal and carry them back to the dining room. "Sorry," I tell Greg. "I had trouble remembering where I put them."

He holds out his hands, and I set them there in a pile. "I need to get your signed permission to search the dorm room," he adds, taking a neatly folded piece of paper from his front pocket. "Would you like me to talk to Jen about it?"

"No, that's okay," I tell him, unfolding the paper and laying it on the table. "She's upset about all this right now. It's a lot to deal with, having just been through the funeral. But I'll go ahead and sign it for you."

He takes a pen from the same pocket and removes the cap, handing it to me. "Was there anything else you took out of the room?"

"Nothing," I tell him, signing my name on the dark line at the bottom of the page.

"All right." Greg bends over and, taking the pen from me, signs next to my name as witness. Then he picks up the paper and refolds it, placing it again in his pocket. We stand there for a moment, listening to the sound of Jen running water and cutting vegetables in the kitchen. "We'll finish the search by tomorrow evening. After that, you're free to clean out the room," he tells me.

I nod slightly, meeting his eyes. "Thank you."

We walk out together onto the front porch, where he turns to me and shakes my hand. "I'm sorry about this," he says, looking past me out at the yard that stretches to the field and down to the river. "Sometimes things just hit you out of the blue. He was a great kid." He sniffs a little, glances at me, then away. For a second I feel the tears come to my own eyes. "If anything else comes up that you think we should see, call me," he says as he walks down the steps off the porch. "Sometimes people find things or think of something else after we've searched."

"All right," I tell him, nodding slightly.

I stand there watching as he opens up the patrol car and sets David's notebooks on the seat. He was a great kid, I tell myself. Greg gets in, wedging himself behind the wheel. I watch as he takes the form I've signed out of his pocket and places it on top of the notebooks. He grimaces a little, then turns to the window with a slight wave of his hand. The patrol car backs down the length of our long driveway, gaining speed once it turns onto the main road.

When I go back into the house, Jen is still standing in the kitchen with her back to me, facing the counter, a pile of vegetables in front of her, a cutting board and a knife. "I'm going to try to meet with the victims' advocate over in the prosecutor's office tomorrow morning," I tell her.

She picks up the knife and slices a carrot into several pieces. "I don't understand why you're doing any of this," she says without turning around.

"Jen, she pushed him."

"You don't know that for sure. I don't understand your reactions anymore. It's like I'm alone in all of this."

I look at the carrot lying on the board in thin, even circles. I can't think of anything to say back to her. I nod my head. I think that, yes, we all are.

PART FOUR

Michael

W H E N W E W E R E kids and ran through the yard to the edge of the field, we were one body, as if we had one mind, the same feelings, one sensation. Following Kay's mother down to the river to collect clay, we would wade into the water and scoop it with our hands, smearing our faces and bodies, then let it dry in the sun.

"Arrugh . . ." The sound of monsters that had crawled out of their caves under the water, dripping gray slime. Kay and David and I lay on the rocks. We pulled one another into the water, splashing.

After I was questioned by the police, I told myself that I hated her. She must have pushed him as part of some warped contract. Both of them thought they could live through the fall or, worse, that they would be together still, drowned, on the other side.

The district attorney grilled me for hours. "What happened after they stopped kissing? Which way was he facing? Where were her hands on his legs? How? Flat or wrapped around? Show us."

I said too many things until it all got distorted:

"I don't know."

"I'm not sure."

"I can't remember."

The more I handled it, the more it unraveled.

My mother refused to come to the meetings with the prosecutor, and when she attended the pretrial hearing, she drove separately from my father and me and sat in the back, not talking to anyone. My father accused her of refusing to help with the prosecution because of her friendship with Kay's mother. That fall, when I went to Bard College, it was a relief to pack everything inside myself and only have to drag it out for the hearings. Later, when I saw Kay in court, I would feel guilty, but during the hearings I got caught up in the current of the proceedings. I was asked question after question about her relationship with David, and I was shown sexual pictures of the two them together. When I was questioned about the sex I'd had with her after the memorial service, I told myself it was mutually initiated and that I had been emotionally confused. I forgot about growing up with her, running along the river, or lying in the grass in the yard and looking up at the sky, the two of us talking for hours.

The hearings were held in a small, drab courtroom during the fall when the leaves were changing. I sat and stared at the large yellow maple outside one of the windows. The sky was a deep blue color, and it was unseasonably warm. I remember walking to the restaurant afterward, taking off my jacket and rolling up the sleeves of my shirt.

I had a calculus test I was trying to study for while I was there and a paper I needed to write. I was missing basketball practice.

I wanted to wrap things up and seal them in a box. The judge was in a bad mood. I heard him ask the prosecutor if this was going to prove a waste of time.

"Tell me what happened, in your own words," he said after I was sworn in. The prosecutor made a move to interrupt, and the judge held up his hand. "Your own words."

I told him about David and Kay taking the acid and how he had stopped on the bridge, how he and Kay had walked out to the middle and started kissing while they were leaning up against the railing. "Then David climbed up onto the railing. She was holding on to his legs when he fell."

"Did she push him? That's the real question."

I glanced at the table where the prosecutor sat. My father was in the row of seats behind him watching me, expectant and grim.

"Yes," I answered.

"Okay." A nod to the prosecutor as I stepped down.

"Don't talk to me about it anymore," I told my father later when we were in the restaurant.

"I'm only trying to tell you that you did the right thing." He was sitting with his arms on the table, leaning toward me, talking in a quiet, insistent voice, the way he would when he was working himself into lecture mode.

"So you say."

I was prepared for one of his big talks on history and morality, but instead he said, "Your mother would tell you the same thing."

I laughed. "She doesn't even want this to happen."

"She doesn't want to think that Kay could do something like this, but when drugs are involved, it's impossible to know what someone is capable of." He paused for a moment, and I watched him drink down his glass of water. "You have to confront some things head-on to preserve what's right. Your mother will see that when this is over. She'll accept it."

"Whatever." I remember leaning back into my chair, glancing around the room, and wishing the waiter would show up with our sandwiches and fries. The train I was taking was supposed to leave in two hours.

"There has to be accountability."

"What if David jumped?" I asked him. "Or what if Kay had jumped first and he didn't? Would you want him prosecuted?"

He was quiet for a minute. "If David had pushed her, he could have been arrested for it," he said carefully.

"But would you have wanted him prosecuted?"

"Possibly. But that's not what happened." His hand wiped across the table impatiently. "Analyzing it like this is pointless. You're too young to have perspective."

"I'm not sure *what* happened anymore," I told him just before the waiter arrived with our food. "It was dark, and maybe I was too tired. I'm not sure I was seeing straight."

"Don't start second-guessing yourself." He reached across the table and put his hand on my arm. "You did the right thing back there in the courtroom."

I was seeing a counselor once a week at the college, but sometimes I couldn't force myself to get out of bed for classes. I had already missed enough basketball practices that my scholarship was threatened, and I was troubled and withdrawn enough that my roommate had asked the dorm for a change.

The waiter came then with the plates, loaded with french

fries and onions. I'd like to think that I didn't argue with my father because I was falling apart. Kay was about to be tried for manslaughter, and I was the main witness. What is awful is that I ate lunch and took the train back that day without trying to say anything more.

Kay

A FEW WEEKS after David's death I was charged with second-degree murder. Officer Townsend drove out to our house and issued the warrant; then my mother took out a loan to post the twenty-thousand-dollar bail, and I was released to wait for the hearing. That afternoon my mother found another lawyer, Barbara Stern, who had a reputation for being both sharp and compassionate. Since the last time I'd been brought in for questioning, my mother had interviewed three other lawyers and had briefly hired someone who specialized in homicide cases and who recommended we pursue plea bargaining if I was charged. Barbara was only thirty and had considerably less experience defending homicide than most of the other lawyers my mother had considered. Her previous cases had involved spousal abuse and a straightforward strategy, usually self-defense. My mother liked Barbara because she so completely believed in my innocence. She reassured my mother that the charges would be dropped when they were presented before a grand jury. As she saw it, there were no solid grounds for my arrest, and she thought I was a victim of an overzealous prosecutor's war against any crime that involved college students and drugs.

When Barbara met with me, she explained that she was preparing for the hearing that would decide whether or not there was enough evidence for the case against me to go to trial. By now there had been a cremation. I kept seeing the shape of David's body or the profile of his face in bed lying next to me.

Everything I was had disappeared by then. This was something Barbara didn't understand about me. She told my mother that she was disturbed by how resigned I was. "The brother claims you pushed him, but your mother insists he jumped," she told me. "Which one is true?"

"He got up on the rail," I answered. "I don't remember pushing him. I was going to jump in with him."

"And then you didn't."

I stared at her for a second, not seeing her. "No. I didn't."

"It looks like there's no real evidence other than the brother's testimony. My guess is that the court won't waste its time."

As it turned out, a few days later the court dismissed the charges of murder because there was no evidence of malicious intent, but it found probable cause for manslaughter, and I was charged formally the next day. During the police interview I'd admitted I didn't remember what had happened and in the same statement had said to them that I was sure I hadn't pushed him. The contradiction they had gotten from me was enough evidence of probable cause, and I could be found guilty of causing someone else's death, even if I hadn't meant it. There was such a thing as unjustifiable risk, and the district attorney claimed that

I had pushed David off the bridge at night into the near-freezing, swollen Connecticut River.

The day after the hearing I made a feeble attempt to do myself in by taking the tranquilizers prescribed for my mother so that she could sleep at night. It was a small bottle, and I took them just before she came home, so that I ended up being driven to the emergency room and having my stomach pumped as a precautionary measure. My indecisiveness stopped me again, and my attempt at suicide just after being arraigned on the manslaughter charges would later be used against me.

I moved through the next ten months as if I were sleepwalking. I had dropped out of college, with no plans for going back. As it turned out, my old roommate, Sara, became the only friend I had during the hearings and the trial. While we had talked when we were roommates about our courses and things going on in the dorms, I had never talked to her about David. Before the spring semester ended, my mother brought back home my things that were still in the dorm room, and a week or so later Sara came to my house with a shirt and a pair of earrings that she'd found. The earrings were ones that David had given me, and as she set them in my hand, I started crying.

"There's the shirt also," she said gently. "I'll just put it on the table."

Then she asked me if I was all right, and we ended up talking most of the afternoon. I told her that I didn't care what happened to me, because I had already lost him. "I want to go to jail," I said. "Part of me wants to be dead."

Unlike my mother and Barbara, she didn't try to get me to

fight against the prosecution. She had experimented herself with marijuana a couple of times, and she knew what the confusion of being high on a drug was like. She had also been in love. The boy she'd been seeing that year had broken up with her suddenly a couple of weeks earlier, and it would be some time still before she got over him. She came to visit frequently that summer, and she continued to visit after the fall semester began. We went for walks and sat up late into the night talking. She was the person I cried with, and she was able to get me out of bed when even my mother couldn't.

That fall there were meetings with Barbara and pretrial hearings. My mother took the sick leave she had accumulated to stay home with me, seeing to it that I went to appointments with the counselor and the psychiatrist she'd found and to the meetings with Barbara. The prosecutor's office had a psychiatrist evaluate me also. It came out that I'd lied during the police interviews. I'd known that David had tried smoking pot on a couple of occasions, and we'd been having a sexual relationship for nearly eight months. I was asked so many times to repeat the events of that night that the details washed away. Had his hand touched my leg as we drove? Had Michael said "you fuck" or "you are such a jerk" when he threw himself back into the car after the train went past? The erasure anesthetized me so that for much of the time after the afternoon when I took the pills, I wasn't aware of feeling anything.

"You are not guilty of killing him," my mother kept telling me. "I am sure you never pushed him." I couldn't remember anymore. I had supported him as he climbed onto the rail, but were my hands there afterward so that we could keep touching, or had I leaned against him? It would have taken little to unbalance him.

Barbara turned out to be right about the prosecutor's agenda. That year he tried six other drug-related cases. My mother, who followed all of them, going so far as to read some of the depositions, reported that character degradation was always a part of his strategy. During the pretrial hearings I was characterized as insecure and devious. I had lied to the police. I was a risk-taker, seductive, and possessive. I didn't know how to set boundaries involving sex.

All of it was public. There was coverage of the case in both the local newspapers and those in Boston. The lawyer told us about a story posted on the news wires. The incident was described conversely as a freakish love pact, a malicious tragedy, a tragic accident, and an example of what could happen when kids experiment with drugs. It was parceled out in articles and editorials as a warning to parents of college students. In the local paper there were enough reports that my lawyer was able to get the trial moved to a different county, but it ended up being scheduled close enough that anyone interested drove the few extra miles to watch the proceedings.

The idea that Michael was the main witness made me doubt anything I thought I remembered. I was sure whatever he said about that night would be the truth. Barbara became increasingly worried as the pretrial hearings progressed. One afternoon when we were in her office, she paced the floor, walking back and forth from the chair I was sitting in to her desk where the folders of paperwork were spread out. It was a bare office, compared to Mr. West's. There were no paintings on the walls, and the bookshelves were stacked with folders.

"Kay, tell me this: Why would you have jumped with him?"

I was quiet for a minute.

"Don't think too much about it. Just answer."

"Because I wanted to be with him."

"You were in love."

I nodded.

"Not even that kind of risk mattered? Not even if you died?"

I shook my head.

"Did you push him?"

"No." I had started crying, a kind of soundless crying that happened often now, in which tears simply ran out of my eyes and I couldn't stop them.

"Your hands were touching his legs when he fell off, and you had taken acid earlier that evening, which is known to distort perception."

"I'm not sure. Maybe I did."

She leaned over for a second so that her face was close to mine.

"You have to be sure about it, Kay. This is what the prosecution will be trying to prove." She turned away from me and walked back to her desk. "Why did you have your hands on his legs when he was standing on the rail?" she questioned.

"I don't know."

"Did you want him to fall? Were you helping him to fall?"

"No. Maybe."

"You can't do this, Kay. Think about what I'm asking. Remember, a one-word answer is best—in this case, no." She stared at me intently. "Why did you have your hands on his legs?"

"Resting there." I wiped at my face. "It was like holding him, touching him."

"Was it sexual?"

"Yes."

"A sexual kind of touch?"

I nodded.

"How were your hands placed there?" She demonstrated with her own hands. "Were they flat, like this, or were you gripping him, like this?"

"I'm not sure."

"Kay." She stood up and moved close to me, brushing against the sleeve of my shirt. "You need to be sure. Think about how they were placed."

I sat there for a moment, thinking. "He was facing the water, and my hands were wrapped around his legs at the knees, holding him there. I don't think I leaned against him." I glanced up at her. "I'm not sure."

Barbara walked over to where my mother sat, gripping the underside of her chair. "You may need another lawyer," she said, pressing her forehead for a minute into the palm of her hand. "Someone who specializes in homicide or manslaughter."

"God, Barbara. I can't stand the thought of that." My mother glanced at me. "She didn't push him. She just needs more confidence. That's hard to get when you've been through everything she has. She needs someone who will present the truth, because she didn't do anything."

"If she was holding him at the knees, she wouldn't have had to lean very hard." Barbara paused, looking at me for a moment. "They've admitted the psychiatrist's evaluation done by the court," she said, picking up a large envelope and handing it to my mother. "This is a copy of it. It states that while Kay has no mental diseases or defects which would have prevented her from understanding the consequences of falling from the bridge, she has a history supporting a motive for the crime. It cites things like the inability to deal with authority figures, and they make an issue of her being unable to establish boundaries in her relationship with David. They claim that her state of mind after David's death wasn't typical. The psychiatrist saw no evidence that she'd begun the grieving process. He says she seemed curiously untouched by everything, including the charges brought against her."

"She was in shock," my mother said, fidgeting with her various necklaces. "She's *still* in shock. How can they twist that up and make it look evil?"

Barbara took out another folder and leafed through it. "And there's the issue of the bruises that were seen by the investigating officers the day after the incident. Kay's never given an explanation for them. The prosecution may try to use them as evidence."

"What do you mean, as evidence?"

"They may try to suggest that there was some kind of a struggle."

"You mean that Kay and David were fighting?" She glanced at me. "That's impossible."

"The jury won't know that. The bruises suggest some kind of physical altercation."

My mother pulled at the necklaces, looking down at her hands. "That's crazy."

"You have to try to see this from a jury's perspective. We need to decide whether or not to use the insanity defense. If Kay were found guilty of manslaughter by reason of insanity, she would be admitted to a mental hospital for sixty days. After that, they'd have to obtain a ruling from the psychiatrist to keep her there."

"Kay's not insane," my mother said. "I don't want her getting committed."

Barbara tapped the folder against her desk. "She'd be there for sixty days; then, chances are, she'd be released. It's preferable to a prison sentence. David's actions were not sane either. They were both influenced by the acid, but I could probably find evidence connected to prior drug use by him to support the existence of a mental history. We would argue that Kay went along with him only because at that moment she was not in her right mind—she ignored consequences."

I got up and walked to the window. The office was on the fifth floor, and from it you could see the courthouse. It was overcast outside, and the century-old stone building looked imposing with its domed roofline and turretlike spires. I'd stopped crying, but my face was still damp. Behind me I heard my mother standing up.

"I suppose we should consider all defensive strategies at this point," she said.

I turned from the window. "I would rather plead guilty," I told them.

"You mean *not* guilty," my mother said quickly.

"No. I would rather go to jail."

My mother put her hand on my arm, gripping it for a

moment. "Barbara's not suggesting that you're actually crazy. She's saying you agreed to something irrational because you were not sane at that moment."

"Then she's suggesting that David was insane or that our relationship was."

Barbara leaned back against her desk. "Kay, think about this some more before you decide. This kind of case is dependent on jury sympathy for the defendant, and there's no other evidence that you didn't push him besides your word, so you will have to testify. The prosecutor will find the holes in your story and inflate them like helium balloons."

"He's dead, Kay," my mother said. I stared out the window, past the courthouse to where the roofs of the downtown businesses stretched against the sky. "Taking the blame for what he did will not get him back."

"If you want to plead that you're not guilty without the plea of insanity, I can work with that," Barbara told me. "But it'll be difficult to support. It'll depend on your story being airtight."

I nodded slightly. Barbara picked up a folder and leafed through a few pieces of paper.

"Tell me again, why did you lie during the initial police interviews?"

"I was scared. I don't know. I wanted to protect him. I didn't want them to know everything."

"You wanted to keep the details about your relationship private?"

I nodded.

"You can't say that on the stand. It will look like you were trying to hide something and create suspicion. Stick with the fear. You were scared. You weren't thinking straight." She paused. "What about the bruises? Can you remember anything? Anything at all?"

I turned around again, staring at the window.

"Kay, were you in a fight or a struggle that night?"

"I don't remember being in one."

"Did you and David fight at all while you were on the bridge? Think hard. It could make a difference. Was he trying to force you to do anything?"

The sun had come out for a moment, and the light moved through the trees next to the courthouse. "No."

"Holding him back could look like pushing him. If there was any kind of unwanted sexual contact . . ."

I turned around and looked from her to my mother, who had sat down again and was still pulling nervously on her necklaces. "There wasn't."

Barbara hesitated for a moment. "Keep the question in your mind. Be sure to tell me if something comes back about it."

During the months before the trial I was in Barbara's office so often, being drilled with questions, that the stacks of books and folders on her shelves and the view of the courthouse from her window began to feel familiar. What exactly had happened that night on the bridge? What was our relationship like? How often had we seen one another? Where had we gone when we were together? She tried to get me to normalize our affair, to play down any extreme love or passion.

"Think about the relationship you had with Michael also. Was he jealous? Are there reasons he might have for lying about what he saw?"

I grew exhausted thinking about it, and the rehearsed scenarios replaced what I could actually remember. At home I took out David's copy of *Hamlet* and read through the notes he'd written. I found a letter he'd once left under my dorm-room door. I tried to remember what his hands felt like.

One evening when I was sitting in the living room staring out the front window after an afternoon of questioning, my mother commented that I would need to get a couple of new outfits, something conservative to wear for the trial.

The session in Barbara's office had been grueling. Barbara had learned that Kevin had been in David's dorm room the day before it was searched, and she had requested a warrant to have their house searched. I was sitting there looking at the house wondering if they had already searched it or would do it the next day. "All right," I answered briefly when my mother addressed me for the second time about the clothes.

"You don't seem to care whether or not they find you guilty," she said. "Manslaughter can carry a twenty year prison sentence. Even if you got out early, you would end up serving some time. You're only twenty years old. This is worth fighting."

I was staring at the snow that had fallen. From the window I could see the driveway to David's house.

"Are you trying to punish yourself?" She leaned over and shook me by the shoulders. "Tell me what is going on."

"I don't know." I stared past her, out the window to where David's house was partially obscured by the snow. It was something the counselor and I had talked around and around, all the ways the guilt could hurt me if I didn't acknowledge it.

"What is it?" my mother asked, her hands on my shoulders,

leveling her face so that it was inches from mine. "Tell me what you think you did. *He* bought the acid. *He* drove the car. *He* stopped on the bridge."

"I said I would jump."

"Kay, think how ridiculous that is. You feel guilty because you didn't kill yourself. He was high. Otherwise he never would have expected that."

"He did expect it."

I felt her grip my shoulders. "I won't watch you throw away your life because of one night's stupidity. Everything is going to depend upon the jury understanding your story, and there's no way to avoid having you testify. Tell me you'll do whatever Barbara advises."

I turned around and stared out the window, my back to her, and agreed softly that I would.

I HAVEN'T BEEN able to forget anything about the trial—the way the judge sat, alternately disturbed and irritated, the expressions of the different members of the jury and the prosecutor whose voice filled the courtroom. Before it began, Barbara drew out the defense strategy on a sheet of paper. The argument she was using rested on the assumption that I had touched David while he was on the railing but had not pushed him, a tactic she called confession and avoidance. I was admitting that I was there when David went off the bridge and that we were touching one another, but Barbara would argue that my actions were not criminal. The rest of the strategy would involve showing that I was a sensitive but responsible individual who had made the mistake of agreeing to take acid and had been overly influenced by love for someone who made a fatal decision.

"Does it make it all right to shove someone off a bridge if you're high?" the prosecutor asked in his opening statement the first morning of the trial. He was a large man who wore dark wide-framed glasses with thick lenses. Harvard-educated, he had moved out to western Massachusetts from Boston a few years earlier, and he spoke loudly and gestured frequently.

"Are you going to send out the message 'get high and you can do whatever you want?' On the night of March sixteenth, Kay Richards took LSD of her own free will. At close to midnight she agreed to ride out to the French King Bridge, where she went with David Sanderson to the edge, overlooking the river. She then assisted him in standing on the rail, from which she pushed him one hundred and forty feet to his death.

"The prosecution will produce evidence which shows that on the night of March sixteenth the Connecticut River was dangerously high, with a water temperature close to freezing. These facts were stated in the local papers two days prior to that night, and Kay Richards knew, like everyone else who grew up living along the river, that the current was always dangerous in the spring, when the level of the water rose. Kay Richards had known David Sanderson since childhood, having grown up as his next-door neighbor. The prosecution will show how she pursued him, starting the previous fall when she moved into the

dorms of the university he had been attending. We will outline
Kay Richards's history of personal difficulties and show how
those difficulties impacted her actions that night.

"The defense may argue that Kay Richards did not understand the risk of jumping into the river, but evidence will show
that any reasonable person would have known the dangers of
jumping from that height into the river. And was Kay Richards
reasonable? I think you will find that she was. Her SAT scores
were above average. She was attending college. There is no history of a neurologically based dysfunction. It is our contention
that she was disturbed, but not at all insane. We will introduce a
pattern of personal problems, beginning with her lack of a stable
family situation and including her improper relationship with
David's brother.

"Kay Richards was a disturbed young woman who knew
fully what she was doing when she led David Sanderson to the
edge of that bridge and pushed him into the river. While you
may end up feeling a kind of sympathy for her, you must not
lose sight of the crime she committed on the night of March
sixteenth. Taking another person's life cannot be excused away.
Her decision to take the LSD that night cannot mitigate what
she did while she was under the influence of a drug. Her actions
involved at worst a warped intent to harm someone she claims
she loved and at best a reckless lack of consideration for his life.
We are confident you will find her guilty as charged of involuntary manslaughter."

The case was being tried in the superior courtroom on the
third floor of the older part of the courthouse. The high-
ceilinged room had a large, rectangular dome at the center of

the ceiling, from which hung a gold-globed chandelier. There was gilded wallpaper with Grecian-looking laurel patterns along the upper edge of the walls, and smaller chandeliers lined each side of room, spaced evenly from one end to the other. The judge's bench was wooden and carved with a pattern of sunbursts or fans. In front of it were two large wooden tables, one for the prosecution and one where I sat with my lawyer. Behind us a railing separated the courtroom from the gallery, two sections of pewlike benches filled with reporters and spectators. Even with all the people, the room was quiet, and the long windows flanking it had panels of stained glass, like a church.

The acoustics in the old room were not good, and when the prosecutor spoke, there was a slight echo. By contrast, Barbara's voice was clear but much softer. She was a small, neat woman. That morning, she wore a dark jacket over a nondescript skirt, similar to the one my mother had bought for me. The argument she began in her opening remarks sounded reasonable, but it was dwarfed by the large, ornate room and the prosecutor's words, which hovered above us in the domed ceiling.

Judge Thompson, who sat listening intently, his chin cupped in his hand, was a black man in his fifties, highly experienced, Barbara had told us, and impossible to read. He had a reputation for being hard on drug offenders, and he was friends with the district attorney who was prosecuting my case. While Barbara was clearly nervous about their association with one another, she had told us that it wouldn't necessarily mean Judge Thompson would favor the prosecution. He had, she claimed, a reputation for being unpredictable but fair.

The jury was made up of seven women and five men. Half of

them had children close to my age, which, Barbara had explained, could end up helping either side, as they might see something of their own child in me and be more sympathetic, or they could end up identifying with David's parents. There were two nurses in the group, a counselor, a retired teacher, and three businessmen.

The prosecution began its case by questioning Officer Townsend. He described the scene that occurred that night when he arrived at the bridge. Michael, he said, had shown him where David had stood on the railing before going over the bridge. There was a dark scuff mark on the railing at that spot from a shoe. Michael had been able to describe in detail how his brother had climbed up onto the railing and how his body had descended into the river. He described the search, how they had looked first with lights and called through a foghorn. When more help arrived, within ten minutes of his getting there, they had taken a boat out onto the water and thoroughly searched the area under the bridge. They had spent the rest of the night and most of the next morning combing the shore and riding the river with motorized scooters, and for several days they had dragged the river and searched the shoreline.

When he was asked to describe how I had behaved that night, he answered that I was distraught. "She wasn't able to answer our questions about what had happened. She became so upset that we recommended Mrs. Sanderson take her home."

"Can you describe the conditions of the river that night?"

"It was clearly up, the way it is every spring, and the current was strong. You could see that even before you got out on the boat. It was moving fast under the bridge. And the water's cold that time of year. It's full of runoff from the melting snow and not much above freezing."

"In your opinion, do most people who live around the river know that the river is dangerous at that time of year?"

"Oh sure. They should, at least. And the French King Bridge is high enough up that a jump from it is always dangerous. The river is so deep and wide there that it would be extremely difficult to swim to the shore. That's something that's well known. Anybody looking over the railing of the bridge can see that."

The prosecutor got out a poster then with some figures on it illustrating the length and height of the bridge and the railing. "Do these figures accurately establish the distance between the parked car where Michael Sanderson sat and the point on the bridge where David stood before he fell?" he asked, pointing to one of the calculations.

Townsend nodded. "Yes, they're correct."

"Did you go out to the bridge at night yourself to establish the visibility from this distance?"

Townsend nodded again. "We went out under similar lighting conditions. Then the other investigating officer stood next to the rail where David and Kay had been and made several gestures with her hands. I sat in the patrol car."

"Were you able to accurately discern her gestures at that distance?"

Townsend glanced out at me for a second before answering. "Yes," he said.

When Barbara cross-examined Officer Townsend, she asked why it had taken him several days after the incident to begin his investigation. She pointed out that David Sanderson's room was left unsearched and accessible during that time.

Townsend slumped in the chair a little and shook his head. "We thought we were looking at an accident," he said. "We were focused on the search and rescue."

"You're a small outfit, aren't you? And you're friendly with the Sandersons."

He glanced in Kevin's direction. "Since I live fairly close by, I know almost everyone along that road. I know the Richardses also."

"Did you coach Michael Sanderson's basketball team for two years?"

He shrugged. "I probably coached over half the kids who play on the high school team at one time or another."

Barbara glanced at the jury, then back at Townsend. "It took you a week to realize that this was a criminal investigation. During that time crucial evidence for the defense could have slipped away. In fact, Kevin Sanderson, the deceased's father, was in David's doom room just hours before you had it cordoned off. Isn't that right?" she asked.

Townsend sat there for a moment, not answering. I saw how tired he looked, and I thought about the week that they had spent searching when I kept thinking they would still be able to find David. "That's right," he said finally. "I was trying to save a life. It's possible that evidence that could have been used for either side of this trial was lost, but I doubt the room searches would have revealed anything."

"It's not your position to make that judgment, is it?"

"No," he said softly before leaving the stand.

Other witnesses brought in by the district attorney included another police officer who had responded to the 911 call and the female officer who had questioned me. They also brought in the psychologist who had evaluated me for the state, and students from college who knew David and me were questioned about the possibility of my using drugs and my relationship with David. Two of the students who had shared David's suite testified that I had frequently spent the night that year in his room. During cross-examination, all of the students admitted that they were only briefly acquainted with me and that except for hearsay, they knew little about me.

The coroner who had performed the autopsy was also examined. He had found the cause of death to be drowning and explained that there was evidence that David's body could have been caught, tangled in debris under or near the bridge. This explained why it had taken several days for the body to surface. There was also a report of the drug level found in David's blood. It was high enough to have affected him, but not high enough to have been the cause of his death. On cross-examination it was revealed that nothing had been found to indicate an injury's occurring prior to the fall.

The sworn statements I had made the first couple of times I was questioned were submitted as evidence of my questionable credibility. But the statement I had made at the end of the second interview was the most damning, as in admitting to not knowing what had occurred I'd contradicted my own statement that I hadn't pushed him. Evidence of the unexplained bruising on my face and arm was also given to the jury. Written reports established that the water temperature had been thirty-nine degrees that night and the river five feet above its normal height. There were also measurements submitted of the height and width of the railing and of the distance between the place where the car had been parked and the center of the bridge where David had climbed onto the rail. A written report described the ease with which someone could be thrown off balance when pushed from behind the knees. Brief statements by neighbors of ours established that people familiar with the Connecticut River did indeed know the dangers of trying to swim in it during the spring.

The prosecutor submitted measurements of the rail David had stood on, three inches across, and he'd had a piece of wood made to those dimensions so that the jury could better picture it. There were also pictures submitted of the actual railing, illustrating the vertical posts underneath the horizontal rail.

It took more than a week for the district attorney to present his case, and against Barbara's objections, he was able to put my mother on the stand. My mother was furious. The morning she got her summons, she pulled Barbara aside as we walked into the courthouse.

"Why do they want me? It's absurd. They can't make me testify against my own daughter, can they?"

Barbara herself was confused about the district attorney's motives. "Try to keep your answers short," she advised. "And you're allowed to say you're uncertain or that you don't remember."

We filed into the courtroom, and I watched as my mother was sworn in. She was wearing a dark skirt, similar to mine, and a cream-colored blouse. One of the bright scarves she always wore was tucked into the neckline of the blouse, a lavender one, and she had on all her rings. That morning she had given me one of her necklaces to wear inside my shirt, a chain with a tear-shaped crystal she claimed would give me strength.

"You've heard testimony describing Kay as having difficulties with authority," the prosecutor began. "Did the two of you fight when she was living at home?"

"Sometimes," my mother admitted. "But not more than other teenagers fight with their parents."

"Ms. Richards, just answer the question, please," his voice boomed. "Is it true that you and Kay fought?"

"Yes."

"What did you fight about?"

I watched my mother turning one of the rings on her fingers. "Curfews, homework—the typical things you fight about with your kids at that age."

"Did you have trouble enforcing rules, as a single parent, without the support of another parent?"

"No," she answered swiftly.

He paused, moving closer to the stand. "Did she break the rules you set?"

"Sometimes, but I don't think that it happened because I was a single parent."

"But"— he hesitated, shrugging—"you couldn't effectively enforce the rules?"

"Not always." My mother glanced at Barbara, confused. "Can any parent . . . ?"

"Did you find it difficult in other ways, being a single parent?"

Barbara stood up before my mother could answer, objecting.

"Single parenting is not on trial, Mr. Prosecutor," the judge commented.

"Correct." The prosecutor crossed the room and briefly examined his own notes. "How would you describe your own relationships with men?" he asked, looking up at my mother.

Barbara objected again. "No relevancy."

The prosecutor took a few steps toward the bench and commented that it would establish a background for my behavior, and the judge told him to proceed with caution. He walked back over to the witness stand. "Have you had a continuous, stable relationship with a man since Kay was born?"

"I don't know what you mean by that," my mother said, looking at Barbara again, then glancing at me. "I was involved with the same person for the past year."

"And before that?"

"I'm not sure."

"Isn't it true that you've had a number of different relationships with various men and that Kay, while she was growing up was exposed to . . ."

There was another objection, and this time it was sustained. I watched my mother lower her head, and I saw the flash of one of her rings as she raised her hand to her face. It hadn't occurred to me before that the relationships she'd had off and on through my childhood were something she could be criticized for, and now that was happening because of me.

The prosecutor was looking through his notes again. "Were you aware of your daughter's drug use, Ms. Richards?" he asked as he set them down and approached her.

My mother shook her head. "I don't know that I'd define experimentation as—"

"Were you aware that your daughter was using LSD on the night in question?"

"No, but I don't think David's parents knew—"

"If Kay had been using drugs prior to that night, is it possible you wouldn't have known about it?"

She hesitated, looking past the table where I sat and then out into the courtroom, and it took me a minute to realize that she was looking at Jen. "I suppose, but—"

"Is it possible, Ms. Richards, that Kay was using drugs before the night in question and you did not know about it?"

"Yes," she said softly, glancing at me.

"So it is possible that Kay was using drugs prior to that evening. Is it also possible that she supplied the LSD that night?"

"Kay has said that she didn't."

The prosecutor turned around and looked at me, then up at the jury. "Has Kay ever lied to you before?"

My mother hesitated. "All teenagers—"

"Yes or no, Ms. Richards?" he said, shaking his head impatiently.

"Yes," she answered in a low voice.

"And isn't it true that she also lied to the police about certain aspects of her relationship with the deceased and knowledge of prior drug use?"

My mother sat there, her head down until the prosecutor repeated the question.

"Yes."

"Did she tell you that she had a sexual relationship with David Sanderson?"

"Not in so many words, no. She didn't choose to confide that in me, but she wasn't being secretive." My mother raised her hand for a second, and I saw the gleam of the rings. She looked at the jury box, then back at the prosecutor. "Kay wasn't capable of pushing someone off a bridge."

The district attorney smiled briefly in the direction of the box where the jury sat. "Ms. Richards, you've just admitted to not knowing about your daughter's drug use or her sexual relationships. Why should anyone believe that you know or don't know what actions your daughter is capable of?"

My mother's gaze swept past him and for a second took in the courtroom. "Because I'm her mother."

JUDGE THOMPSON'S FAVORING of the prosecution had been clear even before the trial began. Motions my lawyer made against the admission of evidence that seemed meant only to degrade my character were denied, as were any motions requesting a delay. Private photographs of us that Kevin had found among David's things were submitted as evidence of the nature of our relationship. When Kevin came to the stand, they were passed among the jurors as he described his own reaction to finding them.

Next he was asked to describe how I'd acted when he and Jen had arrived in their truck after Michael called them from the convenience store. He was wearing a tweed jacket with a shirt and tie, his professor clothes, and I noticed that the entire time he was being questioned, he kept his eyes on the prosecutor, careful not to look past him at me.

"Kay was not upset the next day the way Michael was," Kevin claimed. "She seemed satisfied. She didn't cry, even when we questioned her repeatedly about what had happened. It was almost as if she was content."

"Kay Richards spent a lot of time at your house while she was growing up, isn't that true?" the district attorney questioned, changing directions.

"Yes. My wife often baby-sat for her in the afternoons when school let out and sometimes during the summer when Kay Richards's mother was working. As she got older, she still came over almost daily to see one of our boys."

"How would you describe her relationships with your sons?"

Kevin frowned, crossing his arms in front of his chest. "I was concerned about the effect Kay had on them as they got older. Kay seemed to rebel against authority, and for periods of time she almost lived at our house. We tried to help her, but I was concerned. I worried about the boys' being around her, especially as she got older. Also, her behavior was often flirtatious, and her clothing was suggestive."

Barbara objected, calling the testimony impressionistic and irrelevant. But after hearing it was crucial in establishing a motive, the judge just told them to get to the point.

The prosecutor nodded his agreement. "Were you concerned more recently about David and Kay's relationship?"

"Definitely. When they were home, both at Christmas and the afternoon and night of the incident, they were together almost constantly. David was a very good student, but I was worried that Kay was distracting him from his studying. I thought they were too involved. She especially seemed overly involved."

The prosecutor faced the courtroom for a second. "How do you mean that?"

"She constantly had her hands on him. It was as if she was too sexual, overtly so."

Barbara had stood again, and I heard her objecting. Maybe there was more that Kevin said and I didn't hear it. Judge Thompson leaned forward as the prosecutor approached the bench. "Your Honor, the psychiatric report for the prosecution states that the defendant may have had inappropriate ways of acting out sexual desires. There's an established pattern that the photographs alone point to."

"Counsel, you're done." Judge Thompson's voice was loud enough to be heard by all of us. "Drop this line of questioning, or I'll rule the photographs as inadmissible."

The district attorney walked back to his table and spent several seconds thumbing through his notes. "No further questions," he said finally as he sat down.

Barbara's cross-examination of Kevin was not successful. "Were you friendly with Kay and her mother before the incident?" she asked at one point.

"Yes, I suppose," he answered, staring directly at her.

"Close friends?"

He hesitated for a moment. "We were neighbors in a rather rural setting. We became friends over time because of the circumstances."

"Was your wife friendly with Kay's mother?"

"They were friends," he said, nodding slightly.

"Didn't they talk almost daily, exchanging news?" Barbara persisted. "Didn't your wife frequently visit Kay's mother in her studio talking with her while she sculpted, and didn't Kay's mother help your wife with the work she does for the animal rescue organization?"

Kevin shrugged impatiently. "Out where we live, people often become friends with their neighbors."

"But the point is that prior to the incident, your family was quite friendly with Kay Richards and her mother. Isn't that correct? You sometimes shared dinner together. Your children grew up together."

"Yes," he said hesitantly.

"And now since the incident, since losing your son, that relationship has changed. You've been grieving deeply over the death of your son, haven't you? I mean that would be normal under the circumstances."

The prosecutor interjected noisily with an objection. "Where is this going?" he demanded.

"I'd like to get an answer to a difficult question," Barbara proceeded when the judge allowed her to continue. "Did your grief for your son, which is the natural grief of a parent, in any way color your testimony here today against the young woman your family has befriended since she was a girl?"

Kevin paused for a second and his eyes swept past Barbara to me. "No," he said. "It did not."

I HADN'T TALKED to Michael since David's memorial service. He had left for college that fall, and he hadn't been sitting in the gallery with Jen during the trial. The next day I saw when he walked into the courtroom to testify that he looked older. His hair was cut short, and he was wearing a button-down shirt and tie. He took the witness stand without looking in my direction. Then, before he was asked the first question, he scanned the room, and his eyes stopped on mine. It was the only time during his testimony that he would look directly at me, and for a spilt second it was like we weren't in the courtroom, and I thought of him smiling the way he would have a year ago or calling out something—"Hey, Kay! Let's get the hell out of here!" But his expression was distant, and he turned quickly to the district attorney.

"Tell us about your relationship with Kay Richards," the prosecutor asked him.

"She was one of my best friends since we were kids," he answered.

"Did you and David play with her often?"

He nodded, clearing his throat. "The three of us did a lot of things together. There weren't any other kids our age close by. We played outside mostly, and when we got older, we liked to fish or just hang out."

"And when you were just hanging out, did Kay and David ever act in a way that seemed intimate to you?"

"Sometimes. When we were in high school, I saw them kiss one another." He stared down at his hands for a moment.

"So they had a sexual relationship with each other prior to that night?"

"I think so."

"I need you to tell the court what happened the night they took the LSD. Tell us first how they got the drug and where they were when they took it."

His description of that night, like mine, sounded rehearsed. He said that he had come outside into the yard where David and I were talking about trying acid. We had asked him if he wanted to take it with us, and he had said no, even though David and I had tried to convince him. The two of us had swallowed it down with a can of Coke. Later we had had dinner and stayed around for the party at Michael's house.

"And did they get noticeably high from the drug?"

He nodded. "They seemed kind of spaced out, but they were still talking to people at the party. They weren't totally freaked out or anything."

"Were you worried about David's ability to drive when you got into the car?"

"Yeah, somewhat. We had a fight about it at one point."

The prosecutor glanced in my direction. "Tell me about the drive."

Michael paused for a moment, and I thought he wasn't going to say anything, but then he began to describe in detail what had happened. "First we drove to the railroad crossing. David was out of it, and he stopped on the tracks. I kept telling him to move the car, but he sat there. Then, finally, I got out of the car."

"While you were all three sitting in the car, parked on the tracks, did Kay ask him to move it?"

He looked down for a second, then back up at the prosecutor. "No."

"The train got pretty close, and I could see them still in the car. Then David started it up at the last minute and drove it off."

"It was David's decision to move it?"

His face flushed as he shrugged. "I guess so. Yes. He moved it."

"What happened after that?"

"I was mad, and I wanted to go back home. I wanted to be the one driving, but it didn't seem worth getting into a fight. We argued about where to go. They wanted to drive out toward Millers Falls. We went through the town, and everything was shut down. After that, he followed Route Two to the French King Bridge, and then he pulled over just before we drove across it."

"And where was the car parked?"

"David pulled over to the side of the pavement once he'd driven partway onto the bridge."

"What happened next?"

"David and Kay got out, and David told me to get out." Michael stopped talking, and for a minute the district attorney just stood there watching him. You could hear the sound from the computer where the court reporter was setting everything down.

"Did you get out of the car?" he asked finally.

"Yes."

"What did you do?"

"I walked along the edge of the bridge with them and looked over it into the river. I tried to get them to go back to the car, and they wouldn't. Finally I turned around and walked back while David and Kay went all the way to the middle of the bridge."

The prosecutor nodded, encouraging him. "So to you it seemed dangerous, being on the bridge that night."

"Yes."

"Did David and Kay stay on the bridge?"

Michael looked down at the floor. His voice went so soft that he had to be asked to speak more clearly. "They were standing right at the edge next to the railing, in the middle where it's highest. I heard David shout something. They liked the rush it gave them, like an adrenaline rush or something. I was mad that they wouldn't come back. I got in the car, and the key was still there, so I tried to start it."

"Did you start it?"

"No, not then." He paused for a minute. "After David went over the railing, I started it."

The prosecutor took several steps back toward the observers then turned to Michael again. "What happened before David went over the railing? Where were the two of them standing in relationship to one another?"

"They were close together at the edge of the bridge," he said slowly. "It looked like they were making out, kissing one another. Then David got up on the rail."

"How did he stand on it, facing the bridge or the water?" The prosecutor demonstrated with his body.

"The water," Michael answered.

"Was Kay touching him at that point?"

Michael nodded, staring at the floor somewhere in front of him. "She had her hands on him."

"Where on him?"

"At first it looked like she was holding him, helping him balance or something while he was crouching. Then, as he straightened up above the rail, it looked like she was holding on to his legs."

"Where on his legs? Can you show me on this?" The prosecutor picked up a board from his table, which he explained was for the purpose of demonstration, and carried it over to the witness box, where he held it out to Michael, who took it in one of his hands, wrapping his fingers around it.

"Like this," Michael said. "She had her hands wrapped around his knees."

I saw the prosecutor nod. "Describe what happened next."

Michael glanced out at the courtroom for the first time. He looked somewhere past me. Then he stared at the floor again. "It looked like she pushed him. She kind of leaned into him." It was quiet for a few seconds, so that you could hear the computer keys. "I jumped out of the car. I was screaming at Kay to come back off the bridge, and I ran up there to meet her. When she came back and got in the car, we went to call my parents. She was saying things that didn't make sense, like she wanted me to drive off the bridge."

"What exactly did she say?"

" 'Drive it off the bridge.' Then later she said she was supposed to jump with him."

"Is there anything else you can add about what you saw?"

He thought for a minute. "It seemed to happen slow, the way he went over," Michael said softly. "I was sitting there like I was frozen. I thought I heard him hit the water."

"I have one more question. Have you and Kay Richards ever been sexually intimate with each other?"

He nodded, reddening, and even though I had been told that this would come up, I felt short of breath.

"Can you tell us how that happened?"

"The evening after the service for David, we walked down to the river, and we were talking."

"And then what?"

He shrugged, staring at the floor again. "We ended up having sex there. I was freaked out about everything. I wasn't thinking."

"What happened when you left the river and went back to your house?"

"She wanted me to come with her and drive over to campus and spend the night in her room."

"How did you answer her?"

Michael glanced up for a second, and I thought maybe he saw me. "I told her I couldn't."

"You didn't feel right about being with your brother's girl-friend right after his death?"

"No." He paused. "Kay and I were close friends, but I didn't."

As a recess was called, I stood up and watched him leaving the courtroom with Kevin and Jen and the district attorney. I was thinking ridiculous things, like what we used to yell back and forth to each other when we were running through the fields or hanging out on the bank of the river. He had said that I'd pushed David, and so I knew that I must have.

WHEN WE REENTERED the courtroom, Michael went to the front again and sat in the witness chair. During the recess Barbara had said she would discredit his testimony. My mother had asked lots of questions while I sat there like I had no emotions. I couldn't stand the thought of having to watch him be questioned again. "When we go back in, I'll take him apart" is what I remember Barbara telling us.

When Michael came back up and sat in the witness box, he looked empty, and I recall thinking that by now it was like everything had been poured out of both of us. When I looked at him up there, I didn't feel anything at all.

"Your brother was driving the car, is that correct? All night, including when you stopped on the tracks?" Barbara asked him.

Michael nodded. "Yes."

"So stopping on the tracks was his decision?"

"I guess so."

"You were frightened enough that when you heard the train, you got out of the car. Doesn't it strike you as possibly suicidal that he stopped the car there and didn't move it?"

Michael hesitated, and when the prosecutor claimed conjecture, the judge said he would allow it. After Barbara restated the question, Michael sat there for another moment, and I thought, No, it was not suicidal. Don't tell them it was suicidal.

"I'm not sure," Michael said. "He was tripping. I think he liked taking the risk, but I didn't see it as suicidal."

"He parked the car on the tracks and didn't move it even though a train was coming." Barbara moved in closer to him.

Michael shrugged. "He did move it eventually. David liked to take risks. I think being on the drug made them both less afraid of something dangerous."

Barbara looked at him carefully. "You just said David liked to take risks. That night was he the instigator?"

The prosecutor objected, but Michael was told to answer. Michael glanced at me. "He probably was."

Barbara nodded. "You testified that you asked David to let you drive at one point, but he refused, and I've been trying to picture that. You were walking along the road, and a few minutes earlier he had barely missed being hit by the train. You announce you're walking home. They convince you that it's too far, and you agree to get back into the car. David insists on driving, and you just go along with it."

Michael shrugged uneasily. "I wasn't sure what else to do. David seemed cognizant. He seemed like he was okay to drive."

"Okay after doing acid? Earlier in the evening, before you left the house, did you try to convince Kay not to get into the car, or did you consider talking to one of your parents? After all, this was a dangerous situation."

No, I thought. It didn't seem that way. "Getting my parents involved would have meant telling on David and Kay. I didn't consider doing that. I guess I figured I would go along so that if anything came up, like David being unable to drive or something, I'd be there to drive the car."

"Did you consider that if he was unable to drive, he could end up crashing the car and the three of you—"

I heard the prosecutor object again. The chair I was sitting in didn't seem to be underneath me. I couldn't feel my feet on the floor. "Hypothetical."

Barbara nodded, walking closer to the witness box. "You've testified in the hearing that before you reached the bridge, David had lowered the top of the convertible. Is that correct?"

"Yes," Michael said.

"Why would he do that? It was a cold night. Was he trying to get another thrill?"

Michael shrugged. "I don't know."

"How long did you drive around before stopping on the bridge?"

Michael looked down toward the floor. "I don't know," he said again.

"What did you talk about while you were driving?"

He thought for a minute. Thousands of things, I told myself. Nothing. "I can't remember the actual conversations. Part of the time we were arguing about where we should go."

"What roads did you follow?"

"I'm not sure. David made several turns, and it was dark. Like I said, we drove through Millers Falls."

"When you got out of the car, how far along the edge of the bridge did you walk?"

Michael looked up at her, and I could see the surprise on his face, like for him the whole night was coming undone. This happened. No it didn't—that happened. "What do you mean?"

"Forty feet? Fifty feet? How far did you walk?"

He paused, thinking. "Not that far. Twenty maybe."

"What was said before you went back to the car?"

"We were arguing, because they wouldn't come back with me. I got mad. I think David told Kay to let me go."

"You think." *Yes,* I almost said out loud. *Let Michael go. He's pissed about stuff that doesn't matter.* "And what were you doing when you got back into the car?"

Michael closed his eyes. "I was trying to figure out how to start the engine. I couldn't get the key in the ignition. The roof was still down on the convertible, and I wanted to put it up."

Barbara stepped closer to him. She rested her hand on the edge of the witness box, and when Michael opened his eyes, he was staring past her toward the table where I was sitting. "That's when you claim you looked up and saw David on the railing?"

"Yes."

"You're not certain what was said or what happened prior to your getting back into the car. You were having difficulty getting the car key into the ignition. And you were angry at them for not coming off the bridge with you. How can we be certain you saw Kay push your brother off the bridge?"

He looked down for a moment at his hands. When he looked back up again, I briefly thought that he was going to look directly at me. "That's what it looked like," he said.

"Kay was badly bruised that night. Did you see any indication of a struggle?"

He shrugged, and for a second I thought of myself placing one foot on the rail. "I don't know."

"Are you sure about *anything* you saw that night on the bridge?"

"Yes," he said and then paused, looking out into the court-room, past the table where I was sitting. "I think so," he said finally.

"You were jealous of David, weren't you?" she asked then, her argument taking a turn.

The prosecutor shot up. "Relevance!" he yelled. But the judge allowed it.

Michael sat there for a moment, gazing at the floor. "Were you jealous of David," she repeated, "for his high grades at school and his successes? Were you jealous of his relationship with Kay?"

Finally Michael looked up. "Yes."

"Were you jealous of all of those things?"

He sat there for another moment, staring at her now almost blankly.

"All of the above," he said with a hint of sarcasm.

Barbara moved in close to him, directly in front of the witness stand, and I could see him only partially. "Is that why you testified against Kay?"

"Objection!" the prosecutor called out. "Your Honor, *why* the witness testified is irrelevant. The facts of his testimony stand regardless."

"I'll allow it for now," the judge said slowly. '"But, Coun-selor, get to the point. Establish that it discredits the testimony or drop it."

Barbara turned back to Michael. "Were you motivated by jealousy when you made the decision to testify against Kay Richards? By saying that she pushed him, were you trying to destroy the intimacy between them that you hated?"

The prosecutor had stood up and was objecting again, but Michael was already nodding. "I didn't decide to testify," he said. "My father asked me what I saw. I'm not sure anymore, but it looked like she leaned into him." He lowered his voice, and you could hardly hear the rest of it. "I was always jealous of David," he said.

"Did you see her push him?"

"She had her hands around his knees. It looked like she leaned into him." He glanced past Barbara, for a second, then down at the floor again. "They were practically having sex standing there by the rail."

"Did you hate them?"

Michael nodded.

"You hated and loved both of them?"

"Yes," Michael said.

Barbara turned away from him and walked back to the table where I sat. "No further questions," she said.

YOU START TO think that if you can put the thing together, you'll be able to wake up from the nightmare. I told myself that, listening to Michael's testimony. *You need to hear every word of this.* But the moments when I did wake up were more awful. Michael was the last witness called by the prosecution. Barbara was elated, confident that the case was in the bag. The next morning she began by questioning several character witnesses— two of my teachers from the college, a neighbor, and Sara, my roommate. A medical expert explained the hallucinogenic effect of LSD. The counselor my mother had taken me to testified that the lack of emotion the officers and others had observed after David's death was a result of shock and a sense of numbness commonly seen in people who have been through a trauma. Then, halfway through the day, Barbara told us she had decided to recall Officer Townsend to the stand again.

I remember my mother questioning why she would recall Townsend. There wasn't enough time left during the break for Barbara to explain, but later she would tell us that she had done it mainly on instinct.

"The river runs near your house, doesn't it?" Barbara began.

"Yes," Officer Townsend answered.

"Has anyone you've ever known gone swimming in it before?"

He nodded, shifting in the seat uncomfortably. "Sure. In the summer it's a good way to cool off."

"Who that you know has gone swimming in it?"

"I have, and so has my wife. My kids sometimes swim in it with their friends."

Barbara picked up her notes for a second from the table, then set them down and moved closer to the witness box. "And did you consider it dangerous to swim in the river?"

Townsend shrugged. "Not in the summer. It's a very different situation in the early spring."

"Has anyone you know of ever gone swimming in the river in the spring, say, in March?"

He hesitated. "My son has gone in during May and once in

late April. He had a friend who tried to swim across once. The kid was about fifteen—trying to prove something, I guess."

"Was the risk unknown to your son's friend?"

He thought for a moment, glancing at the judge. "Probably not."

Barbara gripped the pen that was still in her hand. She looked back for a second at me. "When you arrived on the scene that night and began the search, were you certain that David Sanderson wouldn't have survived the fall?"

"No. It seemed likely that he wouldn't have, but we spent quite a long time looking for him."

"How long did you spend?"

"The rest of the night, six and a half hours," he answered without hesitation. "Then we started dragging the bottom. We continued to search the shoreline for five days."

"And during that time, those six and a half hours and even later the next day as you searched the shoreline, would you say that you hoped or expected that David Sanderson could still be alive?"

"Sure, we hoped. The longer the search went on, of course, the less likely that became."

"But for some time you hoped he was still alive."

"Yes," he said grimly.

"And you've said you spent considerable time and manpower searching the shoreline and riding water scooters along the water near the bank. Did you hope to find David there, alive?"

I thought again about those few days afterward. "We were looking for any sign."

Barbara turned to the jury, then looked out into the court-room. "A sign that he might have made it to the shore and gone inland?"

"Anything like that. Of course, we were also looking for a body at that point, especially by morning."

"But," she said, turning back to face him, "it was in the realm of possibility, that David Sanderson could have swam to the shore and pulled himself out of the water."

Officer Townsend shrugged. He moved forward in the chair, and for a moment I thought he was going to stand up. David had said that he was going to pull himself onto the shore, and I had stood by the phone booth imagining that. "It was possible, but we knew it wasn't likely because of the water temperature and the current."

"Possible, in your minds, for him to have survived?"

He paused for a long moment, looking past Barbara until his eyes rested on me. "Yes. I guess it was."

Barbara sat down. "No further questions," she said.

OFFICER TOWNSEND WAS the last witness Barbara called that afternoon. While the prosecutor had taken a week and a half to present his side, she had examined everyone except for me in one day.

I was the final witness called on the last day of the trial. More articles in the newspapers, including stories in the *Boston Globe* and one that was reprinted nationally, had brought in more spectators, and even though it was early in the morning, the courtroom was full and stuffy. In the gallery you could hear people moving around, and it felt like a kind of haze had settled over everything. But as I sat down in the witness stand and was sworn in, the room sharpened with a frightening clarity, and I saw the prosecutor's table and the jury box with each person's face. I saw Jen where she sat in the back row of the spectators' section, and I saw the windows behind her and the outline of the trees through them.

I had rehearsed the questions Barbara was going to ask me numerous times by then, and in front of the jury and spectators I moved through them, dreamily, as if none of what I said was connected to the fact that I had lost him. During the police investigation I hadn't admitted to knowing about David's having tried drugs or to having been intimately involved with him because I was numb with grief. That night on the bridge, when David suggested jumping, I had agreed because it had seemed that we could easily swim across the river. The world was visually distorted. I couldn't tell how far away the water was. We were touching as he climbed onto the rail, and my hands had been touching his legs when he fell, but what I remembered was that he had jumped. I'd been preparing to jump over myself, but then I had hesitated, for some unexplainable reason. I had, Barbara suggested, been governed by instinct.

When she finished, Barbara sat down again at the table we had shared. The room was quiet and heavy. Someone had raised the blinds on the long windows so that the air was flooded with light, and I stared at the lit particles that were floating high above me. For a while the district attorney turned the pages of his notes as if he were looking for something, but when he stood up, he wasn't holding anything. Slowly, he approached the stand, and for a moment rested his hands on the wood, leaning toward me.

"Some of the statements you made to the police on March seventeenth and April fourteenth were false, were they not?" he asked, staring down intently.

"Some of them."

"Would you tell the court which statements of yours were untrue?"

"I knew that David had tried drugs in the past."

"And didn't you also lie about your relationship with him? When asked if the two of you were intimately involved, didn't you answer that you were not?"

"Yes," I answered, the words Barbara had made me repeat so many times circling in my head.

"Did you read the statements before you signed them?"

"Not completely. I glanced through them."

"But you do read English?" He shrugged a little, adjusting the jacket of his suit.

"Yes."

"And you knew that this was your statement?"

"Yes," I answered, remembering the room where I had been questioned and the face of the female officer. "They told me it was."

"You knew it was important, and no one rushed you or stopped you from reading it?"

"I knew, and no one stopped me."

He glanced at the jury. "When asked about the nature of your and David's relationship, did you understand the meaning of 'sexual'?"

"Yes."

"But you told the police you and David had just been going out with each other. That you had kissed."

I sat there for a moment. *Make it clear when he questions you that you were overwhelmed and frightened during the investigation,* Barbara had said. "Yes," I answered.

"When really you were lovers, having participated numerous times in sexual intercourse."

Numerous times, I thought, remembering for a second his body lying asleep against mine. "Yes."

"Isn't it true that you wanted to downplay the relationship? Didn't you want to make it seem that you and he weren't as closely involved with one another as you were?"

Behind him Barbara stood up about to make an objection. "I didn't want everyone knowing about it," I answered, before she could speak.

"Objection," she called out. "Leading the witness." But the judge overruled it.

"How often did you sleep together the last month he was alive? Twice a week? Five times a week?"

"Objection. This line of questioning is irrelevant." I took a breath. I thought how you wake up and then it is all so real, almost crystalline.

"I'll allow it as long as it goes to establish the relationship between the defendant and the deceased." I heard the judge sweep his arm across the table, and when I glanced up, he was looking at me. The prosecutor had repeated the question.

"Five or six times, I guess," I answered.

"Did you ever discuss marriage or your future together?"

One night we had planned it out. We would find an apartment to share in another year, and we would talk our parents into it. *"We'll travel,"* David had said. *"We'll go over to Europe together during the summer."*

"Yes."

"And this was information you wanted to conceal from the police report?"

I could see Barbara, shaking her head a little at first, trying to signal me, then lowering her eyes to the table. "Yes."

"You knew that this information would make you more of a suspect in his death, would call attention to you by suggesting a motive, didn't you?"

"Objection," Barbara said, standing.

The prosecutor glanced at her as the judge said sustained. "You've testified that David Sanderson supplied the LSD the two of you took on the night in question, but as Michael Sanderson didn't know where the drug had come from and no drugs were found in either of your rooms, there is nothing to corroborate your story. Did you supply the drugs that night, Ms. Richards?"

"No, I didn't."

"Was it your intention to get David Sanderson high?"

Barbara was calling out an objection again.

"Withdrawn," the prosecutor said quietly with an impatient wave of his hand. "I'll move to another point." He backed away from the stand and paced for a minute. I thought how it didn't matter, how I could go on answering his questions and then I could go to prison.

"You testified this morning that you were in love with David Sanderson," he began, stopping directly in front of the witness stand, looking at me. "So in love that you agreed to jump off a bridge with him into the river."

"Yes," I heard myself saying.

"You had known him since early childhood? The two of you and his brother, Michael, had grown up together?"

"Yes."

"And you and David had begun having a sexual relationship while you were both at college?"

He stared at me expectantly for a moment, and I thought about telling him that it didn't matter, none of it mattered anymore. "Yes."

"You indicated that you were so in love with him that you would do whatever he suggested."

"Yes."

"Such as taking a drug like LSD, then riding in the car with him even though you were high?"

"I didn't think clearly about the danger of riding in the car."

"But you agreed to take the LSD. Correct?"

"Yes."

"Of your own free will?"

It was all of my own free will, I thought. "Yes."

"You also agreed to stopping at the railroad crossing on the tracks, didn't you?"

Had I asked him to move the car? It seemed like I had. "Yes."

"In fact, you egged him on, knowing it was dangerous, didn't you?"

"I didn't."

"Instead, you expect us to believe that you loved him so much that you allowed him to jeopardize your lives by stopping on the railroad tracks, and that later that night when he said he was going to jump off the bridge—which was clearly a very dangerous act, especially in March, when the level was high and the temperature was close to freezing, a fact that had been drilled into you since you were a child—you readily agreed to help him?"

I looked out at all the faces—my mother's, Barbara's, the people I knew and didn't know, Kevin and Jen. "I thought he could swim to the side."

"And why would someone want to do that?" the prosecutor asked, motioning his confusion to the jury. "Why would someone want to jump into freezing water from that height and try to swim to the side?"

"Because it would be exciting."

"*You* thought it would be exciting," he said, emphasizing the "you."

I took a breath and my body expanded with it. I thought, There is nothing to do but say it all, and it doesn't matter what happens later to me. "Yes."

"So you helped him?"

I nodded slowly. "I helped him steady himself on the railing."

"Because it would be exciting." He paused, taking a step toward me. I could see the sweat that had formed on his face and the small crease on the collar of his shirt. "Exciting to watch him fall off the bridge. Would that be a kind of thrill?"

In the dark, somehow with his hands in my clothes, I had wanted that. "The whole thing would be."

"You like to do exciting things, don't you, Ms. Richards?" he said, stepping back from me again and glancing at the jury. "You like to take risks. You agreed readily to take the LSD while Michael did not. And you stayed in the car while it was on the tracks. Is that correct?"

Barbara stood up, objecting, and the prosecutor turned to the judge for a second, gesturing his annoyance.

The judge nodded at me. "The defendant will answer."

"Yes," I told him.

"Did you enjoy taking risks when you were with David?"

"Sometimes."

"Since David is dead, it's impossible to know whose idea it was to jump from the bridge, isn't it, yours or David's?" He paused for a split second, glancing at the judge. "Withdrawn." He walked back to his table and paged through his notes. Except for the sound of someone coughing in the gallery, the courtroom was quiet. I could see my mother in the strange dark clothes, the bright scarf her only concession, staring at me. After a few minutes the prosecutor looked up. He still had one of the pages in his hand.

"After Michael went back to the car, you and David stood by the edge of the bridge. What happened?"

"We kissed one another," I said quietly.

"Did you embrace?"

I looked down at my hands, white against the dark skirt. Nothing about them looked as if they belonged to me. "Yes. At least we were very close physically."

"Your bodies were touching?" He dropped the paper and walked closer to the witness stand.

"Yes, they were."

"In a sexual way?" he asked, stopping in front of me.

"Yes."

"Who initiated the sexual contact?"

"I'm not sure. I guess it was mutual. We both initiated it."

"The investigating police officers submitted evidence of extensive bruising on your face and arm observed the day following the incident. Was there a physical struggle between the two of you?"

I thought about David standing next to me, our hands under each other's clothing, how I couldn't stand now to remember what it had felt like. "No."

"So you don't remember any kind of physical struggle which could have caused the bruising."

We stared at each other for a moment. "There was no struggle," I said finally.

"So it's your claim that you were standing by the bridge, kissing David with your bodies touching, and then he got onto the railing. Is that right?"

"Yes," I said, thinking how this reduced it, how in the end all of our actions could be reduced to a string of words.

"Were your bodies still touching at this point?"

"Yes. They were."

"You were holding on to him?"

Yes, I thought, and then Barbara made an objection. "Leading the witness."

"Sustained," the judge called out. "Restate the question."

"How were you touching once he was up on the rail?" the prosecutor asked.

"My hands were on his legs."

"Let me picture this. He was crouching above you on the rail, and you were standing behind him. Which way were you facing?"

"We were facing the water."

"And you had your hands on his legs? Why?"

I thought for a moment, and the words that I had been made to say over and over again in Barbara's office weren't in me anymore. "To help him balance," I answered finally. "Or just to be touching still."

"Were your hands stretched flat against his legs, or were your fingers curved around his legs at this point?" he asked, demonstrating.

"They were curved," I said with a kind of certainty.

"Given the size and the rounded shape of the railing, it would have been difficult for him to have stood up on it by himself, wouldn't it?"

"Yes, I suppose so."

"And had David told you already that he was going to jump?"

"Right before he started to get up on the rail."

"What did he say?" His finger waved in the air, marking the point.

"'We can jump off together. We'll swim to the side. I'll go first and . . .'" I swallowed hard, but the words stayed stuck.

"And what, Ms. Richards? 'I'll go first and . . . '?"

"'And you follow.'" I looked out into the room, and I imagined him listening. "'I'll be there.'"

"You've testified in the pretrial hearing that he stood up on the rail facing the water. Did he get up slowly? Did he, for example, crouch there for a moment to get his balance and then slowly straighten, or did he stand right up on the rail?"

"He got up slowly," I said carefully, describing what I hadn't been able to see completely since that night. "He crouched there for a while, holding on to the rail, and then he slowly straightened."

"And how were you touching him at this point? Were your hands on his legs?"

"He was facing the water. I had my hands around his knees."

"Was that when the struggle occurred, Ms. Richards? Was he attempting not to fall from the middle of the bridge into the river when—"

I heard Barbara objecting as the prosecutor, annoyed, waved her away. "All right. What were you thinking at that moment, Ms. Richards, when David Sanderson stood on the railing with your hands around his legs? That moment when you could have held him back or pulled him down off the rail or tried to talk him out of jumping into the deepest part of the river when the level of the river was high enough that the current was too strong to swim against and the water temperature was just above freezing?"

"Objection, Your Honor. That is all supposition."

"Just ask your question, Mr. Prosecutor."

"Ms. Richards, what were you thinking?"

I closed my eyes for a moment and tried to forget about all of them—the prosecutor who wanted me to admit to a fight, Barbara who was disappointed, and my mother who was frightened. "I wasn't thinking anything. Everything looked distorted. The water seemed closer than it was. The river didn't look that wide."

"Were you hoping he would jump? In your state of mind, did you want him to jump?"

"Yes," I said, looking at him directly. "I wanted both of us to. It seemed like it would be . . ." I stopped for a moment, and he moved a little closer to the stand, placing one hand on it.

"What would it be, Ms. Richards?"

"Exciting."

The prosecutor stepped back and looked at the jury. "You were standing there, your hands around his legs, watching him slowly straighten up on the railing and thinking it would be exciting when he went off it and fell into the river."

"I was thinking or feeling that it would be exciting when we both did."

He nodded some sort of agreement and fixed his gaze on me. "I want you to think carefully about what you are saying and remember that you are under oath. Michael testified that he saw David straighten up slowly to a standing position, just as you've now testified, and that your hands were around his legs. Were your hands like this?" He gestured, demonstrating. "So that your thumbs were against the insides of his knees and your fingers were cupping the kneecaps?"

"I think so. I'm not sure."

"You're not sure." He glanced around the courtroom, then

back at me. "You were high from the LSD still, making it difficult to remember accurately what you did and did not do. But
you do know that your hands were around his knees. And you
were helping him to jump, because the idea of that excited you."

I looked at my mother, who was watching me as if she knew
she couldn't stop any of this. "Yes."

"As we've established earlier, the knees are a vulnerable point.
It's especially easy to make someone fall by pushing on them,
even the slightest bit. That would be especially true given the
precarious nature of the rail. Do you understand that?"

"I do. I didn't know it then."

The prosecutor walked toward me. He stopped just in front
of the witness stand. "Did you lean into him? To help him over,
to create the excitement you wanted?"

"No."

"Objection." Barbara was standing. She looked at me, then
motioned to the judge. "He's leading the witness."

"I'll allow it," the judge said slowly. "Continue."

The prosecutor rested his hands on the edge of the box.
"You've said you wanted him to jump off the bridge. Isn't it
true that you pushed him, that you leaned hard into him, as hard
as you could, as he was getting his balance? The bruises on your
arm and face could have been from that struggle, couldn't they,
as you tried to shove him from the rail?"

I shook my head a little, almost confused. "No, there wasn't a
struggle. I didn't fight with him."

"But you did push him, didn't you? You leaned into him just
when he had his balance and could have chosen to step back
down?"

"I don't think so. I'm not . . ." Around me the room wavered unsteadily, as if we were all underwater. "I'm not sure really what happened."

"You're not sure what you did at that moment," he said quietly, his hands resting in front of him lightly on the edge of the witness stand.

"No, I'm not sure," I heard myself saying. "I was going to jump with him."

"But then you didn't. You watched him fall, and you walked away."

I glanced at Barbara and at my mother. This was another kind of betrayal, I thought. "Yes. I don't know why I didn't jump off. I thought I would."

"At that point, as he was standing on the rail, did you still think you would both be able to swim across? Looking out at the river, did that seem possible?"

I stared past them all, past the jury and the spectators, past the windows where the dark tree trunks marked against the sky. "No."

"Excuse me?"

"No," I said, looking back at him. "It didn't seem possible."

"And when he was standing on that rail, you leaned against him, didn't you?"

"I could have," I answered, looking at my mother's alarmed face.

"Did he fall for a long time, Ms. Richards? Did you see him hit the water?"

"Yes." It felt as if the room had disappeared, and I was saying whatever I was saying without any feeling or awareness. My mother would tell me later that that was when I started crying. "I saw him against the darkness. Because there was a streetlight next to us. I watched him fall, and he hit the water."

"What happened next?"

"I stepped away from the rail."

"You had helped him to jump, and then you stepped away?"

"Yes," I answered.

The prosecutor walked toward his table. I saw him pick up a sheet of paper and set it back down. It was quiet except for the sound I made crying. He turned around after a minute and stood there staring at me. "No further questions," he said softly.

THE JUDGE CALLED a recess, and somehow I left the stand and walked out of the courtroom. "People will say anything if they get broken down," Barbara commented resignedly later. "The jury will realize that."

I didn't care what the jury realized. The moment of watching David still played in front of me. I had stood there by the rail. Then I had turned around without going with him.

I followed my mother and Barbara out of the courthouse and into the blinding sun. Several reporters were there asking questions, along with a camera crew for the local news station. "Exciting." The word came back to me. I saw the outline of his body against the bright air.

That afternoon, following the recess, when the closing arguments took place, I was emotionless. "Composed," one reporter would say about me. "Resigned," another would comment. I can't remember much of what the prosecutor said. Later I read that he summarized my testimony, focusing on my admission under oath that I had pushed David and emphasizing my unreliability. Because my hands were clasped around David's knees, even the slightest movement from me, he insisted, would have been enough to plunge David to his death.

By the time Barbara gave her summation, it was late in the day, and I was past exhaustion, both emotionally and physically. It had been months since I'd slept much, and when I had, I'd sunk so deep that an alarm clock had not been enough to wake me. I'd been dragged through the two weeks of the trial, not caring what the outcome was. Now that I'd given my testimony, a conviction seemed appropriate. I only wanted the whole thing finished.

"When Kay Richards took LSD last year on March sixteenth, she did it because David Sanderson had convinced her to. When she got into the car and drove out to the railroad tracks and sat there while an oncoming train just missed hitting them, she did so because David decided to drive and told her to get into the car, because David decided to stop on the tracks. And when she got out and walked along the edge of the bridge overlooking the Connecticut River, she did it because David stopped the car there and convinced her that she should walk with him."

Barbara stopped for a moment, glanced at me, then faced the jury again. "My client has testified that her hands were on him and she leaned into her hands as he fell off the bridge, but there is no real proof that she shoved him. If she had her hands placed on his legs, around his knees, as she has testified, while he stood balancing precariously on the rail, any slight movement from Kay or David could have caused a loss of balance. The fact is, David Sanderson had climbed onto the rounded three-inch rail himself, after convincing Kay Richards to commit yet another dangerous act, but this time she did *not* go along with him. For some reason she says she doesn't fully understand—perhaps because of some innate instinct of self-preservation—she did not end up jumping. Instead, she turned away at that crucial moment and walked back to the car.

"Is it fair, then, to punish her because she was not also able to save David? Because she was unable to save him from himself? It could be argued that she should have said no earlier in the evening—no to the acid, no to the car ride, no to getting out of the car on the bridge. The only eyewitness, Michael Sanderson, has admitted that his own jealousy motivated his testimony. The district attorney has used Michael Sanderson's unreliable testimony and the hearsay of various acquaintances to create an unfair picture of a man who was maliciously pursued, but the simple truth is that both David Sanderson and Kay Richards were in love with each other. Kay Richards was in love with David, and people do things they later regret when they are in love. Other than using the illegal substances, there was no crime committed in her being unable to say no to him, or for that matter in any of her character weaknesses stemming from immaturity, which the prosecution has gone to extreme pains to present.

"Kay Richards went along with David Sanderson. He drove the car. She sat on the railroad tracks because he stopped it there. At one point he put the top down, even though it was cold that night. If everything had gone the way David directed it, we would have two deaths instead of one. If Kay Richards is guilty of anything, it is only of not having jumped herself after agreeing with David that they would do it together. It was David Sanderson's decision that night to jump off the French King Bridge into the Connecticut River. It was his own misjudgment, due perhaps to the effects of the drug, which she claims he had supplied himself with and taken at his own initiative. Kay Richards simply went along with the events of that night. She did not try to argue with her lover." Barbara paused. She stepped back toward our table, looked at the judge, then back at the jury. "You must find her not guilty of involuntary manslaughter."

Barbara sat down next to me, and we waited. The courtroom was quiet. You could hear people shifting in their seats in the gallery. Someone stood up. As it turned out, the judge's instructions to the jury were lengthy, and in a strange way they would end up determining the outcome. "I have several items for your consideration," he began, and something in the deep tone of his voice drew me from the place I'd been drifting. For a second I thought he was going to hand down a direct verdict—guilty as charged. Then I realized he was just pulling us swiftly along, as if the course he followed were inevitable.

"First of all, you must understand that the fact that the defendant's state of mind might have been altered by the drug she had taken cannot enter into your consideration of her innocence or guilt of the crime she is accused of. The ruling pertaining to manslaughter prevents this by stating that if a defendant doesn't realize that her actions are risky because of intoxication or an altered state due to voluntary use of a drug or substance, she is guilty of the recklessness causing the crime."

He glanced down for minute at his table and picked up a sheet of paper. "Second, you should know that Model Penal Code 210.5 states that if someone causes another person to commit suicide by force, duress, or deception, she can be convicted of manslaughter. In a previous ruling, the players of a game of Russian roulette were convicted of involuntary manslaughter when one of the players was killed.

"Third, and this is a complex but important distinction." He paused, glancing at me, then looked back at the jury. "Involuntary manslaughter, as you know by now, is a homicide unintentionally caused. However, in order for the defendant to be liable, the prosecution must prove beyond reasonable doubt that the defendant knew of the risk involved. The defendant may testify that at the time she did or did not realize the risk involved, but the jury may choose whether or not to believe her."

Copies of these instructions were handed out, and the jury members were taken away. As it turned out they would deliberate the rest of the afternoon and that evening, so the verdict would not be given until late the next morning. When we left the courthouse, my mother insisted that we go out with Barbara for dinner, even though I said I couldn't eat.

"We can appeal if we have to," Barbara told us once we'd sat down and ordered from the pasta menu she seemed to know well. "The case is unusual enough that there are plenty of grounds for it."

I stared blankly at the salads and bread the waitress put down in front of us.

"Where would she be sent if it comes back as guilty?" my mother asked.

"The judge rules on sentencing. Probably somewhere with minimum security. But don't think about that yet. I'm expecting it'll be not guilty." She smiled at me, but the lines of her face were grim. If the verdict was guilty, I would refuse any attempts to appeal it.

After we got back from the restaurant, my mother and I stayed up until the early hours of the morning. She brought out pictures I had never seen, taken years ago, of her with my father. He was tall and thin with a beard and long dark hair, similar in color to mine. In one of the pictures he was wearing a sweater knitted with brightly colored stripes. His arm was around my mother, who was pregnant with me, and he was laughing.

"That's the car he drove to California." She pointed to a picture of an older off-white VW bug with a sun roof, which he was waving from.

"Maybe he never made it all the way there. For a while I tried to contact him, thinking he would want to see you. His parents lived in Chicago, and I had their address, but they didn't answer the letter I sent them." She paused. "You think you know someone, and then they do something you could never understand."

"My father?" I started to ask, and then it occurred to me that she could mean any of us—me, Jen, Michael, or Kevin.

After a time she put on water for tea and coffee. Then she

found a radio station that was playing old jazz tunes and pulled me from my chair and insisted on dancing with me.

"We used to do this at night when you were little, before you went to bed. You always loved it."

Around us the music swelled until it spilled from the room, filling the rest of the house. My mother's body moved with mine, awkward at first, then more smoothly. It seemed to go on for a long time, the swell of notes, our bodies pulling away, then drawing in to one another. For a while I was conscious that I was crying; then that slowed as the music did, and I thought how I would carry the crying inside myself, folded away, the rest of my life.

The next morning we were awakened by a phone call from Barbara telling us to be at the courtroom by eleven. My mother made a breakfast I didn't eat. She talked incessantly about inconsequential things, like the weather, as if we were getting ready for a trip to the store.

At quarter past eleven, when I stood to hear the verdict, everything in me stopped, the way it had almost a year earlier when I was standing at the edge of the bridge watching him fall. Morning sun came through the stained glass panels on the window, so that the ceiling seemed higher and more expansive, marked with pieces of color. The courtroom was almost empty compared to the day before, but it had the same hushed quality that had been there when I gave my testimony.

"We find the defendant not guilty of the charges of involuntary manslaughter," the jury foreperson read.

The gallery was instantly noisy, and I was aware of people standing and talking behind me. The prosecutor closed his briefcase. Then, as my mother and Barbara hugged me, I could see

Jen behind us getting ready to leave. She paused for a moment before turning around, and her eyes met mine. There was no anger in them, just a kind of remote sadness.

"Thank God," my mother whispered as Jen walked out of the courtroom, and it took me a minute to realize what she meant. I already knew that not guilty would be the harder of the two for me to live with.

Later it would be explained to us that the jury had focused on the last point in the judge's instructions. The river, they had decided, could not be defined, beyond any doubt, as a known danger. There was clear evidence in retrospect that it was dangerous, but there was not enough convincing evidence that I had known that night that it was dangerous.

Had the judge, as Barbara suggested, turned against the prosecution and given the jury the information to find me not guilty because of the district attorney's unfair attacks against me? It was impossible to know. The other two points of instruction had presented reasons to find me guilty. The irony is that I *did* know about the danger of the river. I grew up hearing the warnings each spring. I understood the danger of falling from such a height and I had heard someone comment on the raised level of the water at the party. Oddly, it was something the prosecutor had not questioned me about very thoroughly.

When we walked out of the courtroom, there were reporters waiting, and someone took my picture.

"How does the verdict feel?" someone asked, pressing against me. "What do you think you'll do now?"

A man pointed a microphone in my direction. "Was it what you expected? Are you going back to college?"

That evening, after the barrage of calls forced us to stop answering our phone, my mother insisted we go away. My grandparents owned a house on Cape Cod, and the following afternoon we left to stay with them for a few weeks. Much of it had come back to me by then—the heightened sexual sensation, my hands against his legs as he stood on the bridge, the feeling of my body leaning into his, the absolute clarity with which I believed that both of us would jump. Then the confusion of being in the car and not knowing why I wasn't with him. And I could remember also the way in which everything was altered by the acid and how it had made simple things beautiful, like the film of dust on a bowl or the skin of an apple. I could remember the party earlier that night, with people moving all around me talking, their conversations a kind of giant web. I could hear David's voice again in the center; I could see how he had spun the web.

I also thought about what had happened with Michael after the memorial service. During the trial I could have claimed he had raped me, but when he pushed me down against the bank and took off my clothes, I'd felt a kind of relief, as if it meant I hadn't already lost everything.

My mother and my grandparents were patient with me. They didn't expect me to say anything while we were there. I walked along the beach with my mother or grandmother the way I had when I was a child and we visited during the summer. I sat in the kitchen while they steamed crabs and went out with my grandfather in his small boat, puttering along the bay and stopping for an hour or more to throw out a line.

I could walk through the small cottage or along the coast as reflection, as if I had disappeared. "She'll come back," I heard my grandmother comment. "When she's ready, she'll come back."

THAT FALL MY mother tried to convince me to enroll at the university again. When I wouldn't, she got me to accept a job that was offered to me working in a small store owned by Sara's mother, selling stationery and notebooks and cards. It was several months before I felt able to do anything like drive, and in the evenings Sara or my mother would pick me up from work. Sometimes, on the way home, we would stop for dinner, or on the weekends, if Sara didn't come over to visit, my mother insisted on the two of us going to the movies. She taught me what she knew about gardening, and during the winter I helped her paint the kitchen the pale yellow color of corn. Not stopping for too long, that was her philosophy.

She and Jonathan had quit seeing one another that summer before the hearings began, and she and Jen never became friends again. While she has cultivated other friendships in the last few years, I haven't seen her become close to anyone. She's continued to teach her classes and make her sculptures, which more and more frequently find places in exhibits.

Two years after the trial I enrolled in the technical school, and for three years now I've worked at the hospital. Even after I've turned off the screens and put away the films, I can't get out of myself. Everything resembles the images from the machines—the food I cook for dinner, the shadows on the TV.

I live in an apartment in Allston, one bedroom with a small living room and kitchen in a large, older building with noisy elevators and grates on all the windows. Like a hole you can curl up in. There's a TV set, a radio, and a CD player. A piece of food, a slice of sound. The walls are pale gray, the color of old paper. There's a small couch, a table I painted blue for eating off of, a wicker chair, a box of tissues.

I have a canary, which I keep in a cage that hangs by the window, and in the evenings I let it out to fly through the rooms, singing near the ceiling and by the windows, landing on the sill or counter. Light settles on the walls and furniture, and the rooms feel fragile and delicate, as if everything could be blown away.

My mother says I need to move on. She recommends support groups and the distraction of work. I put Kee-Kee back inside her cage, shut the clasp on the door, and get ready for bed. My body has become foreign. I've lost weight, cut my hair short.

For a while I dated someone I met at the hospital. We used to drive to the ocean on the weekends, and we'd go out for dinner after work, or to a movie. I avoided mentioning David to him. We had a lot in common—our work in the lab, friends, a certain hermitage. He sometimes spent the night in my apartment.

"You're haunted by something," he said just before we split up. "Whatever it is, you won't let anyone past it."

Sometimes I picture David and myself together like other couples I see, going out shopping or talking about starting a family. My mother says that when you are young you do things that are at once both wonderful and destructive. You fall in love in a way that is complete and self-absorbed, and it's hard to believe that drugs or anything else can hurt you.

In the mornings I let Kee-Kee out of her cage while I shower and dress. I ride the train, then walk the three blocks to the hospital, down the hallways into the rooms for radiology. I read through the list of cases and set up the machines, a kind of removal, a way of being cloistered.

Sometimes he still steps out of the past, quiet and whole. When he opens his arms, I want to go inside them.

"You need to move forward with your life," my mother tells me.

His body is full of light. He closes his arms around me, and it fills my heart.

PART FIVE

Kevin

THREE WEEKS AFTER the end of the trial, the death certificate comes in the mail: "Drowning by a drug-influenced accident or suicide." It lies on the kitchen counter, the last piece.

It's nearly evening, the light quiet and pale. I can hear Jen in one of the rooms, packing. I've taken a teaching position at a college in upstate New York. It's a step down and pays less, but I can't live here anymore. Sometimes during the trial, when I went to teach a class, there was a reporter waiting for me outside the building.

"Could I have a word with you about the trial? Is it true that you made the request to the prosecutor's office that Kay be indicted? How long have you known Kay Richards and her mother?"

They would stand by the classroom door or near my office or outside the courtroom. One evening the crew for a local news channel was parked on the road in front of our house. My students read about it in the papers and saw the clips on TV. The media glamorized what happened. "A love affair with tragic consequences," one of the articles read.

Jen has joined a couple of different support groups for parents who've lost a child. She spends hours on the phone listening while others tell their stories. At night I shut the door to my study. I've finished most of the chapters of the book I've been writing. The problem with writing about history is that so often the tracks have been erased. Few lives are recorded, and sometimes the historians who've come before you have wiped out the traces of what they didn't want to see—a racially charged incident or a battle whose outcome they didn't agree with. You're left having to reconstruct, unable to grasp motive or intent.

On one of the corners of my desk I keep a folder that's filled with the notes I collected on the prosecution's case and photographs of the bridge. The study of history is the pursuit of truth—that's what I tell my students. But it's very slippery, even in the present tense.

"Jen," I call out now, climbing the stairs, looking for her. There's the scrape of a chair moving across the floor and the sound of something being set down. Since the trial ended, she's kept busy doing work for her friend Sandy the veterinarian. I try to remember the last time we slept together. I'm like a field, I tell myself, empty, washed with light. I've stopped eating unless I have to. There are nights when I don't sleep.

"Jen?" I call again.

That last day of the trail, after the verdict was read, we drove home together. "What did you get out of this?" she asked me as we got into the car.

she gave him the drugs we found in his room or if she sold them to him. Absolutely none."

She turns slightly in her chair and looks out the door to his room for a minute, then back at me. "You think you can destroy evidence to support your version of what happened. What if you're wrong?"

"I wasn't. She confessed."

"But there was no maliciousness in what she did."

"Manslaughter doesn't involve malicious intent."

She stares at me for a moment in frustration. "What if her story is true? What if he supplied the acid and talked her into everything and she went along with it, thinking that they would both jump? It was a tragedy, but how can you say that it was her fault?"

"Because he's dead. And she has lied so many times there's no way to know if he supplied the drugs and talked her into everything."

She narrows her eyes. "You lied also."

I sit there looking at her, trying to come up with an answer. Sometimes the end justifies the means. My lie supported a greater moral reality. I was trying to protect my son.

Her face is drawn, her eyes hard. I find her almost unrecognizable. I remember that when we first found out Kay and David were seeing each other, I tried to talk to her about it. "Their relationship doesn't bother you?" I asked her.

"You can't control who your children fall in love with" was her only answer.

"It wasn't entirely Kay's fault," she says now. "It happened because of all of us. Because David bought acid and brought it home. Because we were so busy with the party we didn't notice that they had taken a drug. Because Michael got mad at him on the bridge and didn't try to stop him. And because Kay agreed to go with him. She was the last thing, the last reason no one stopped him. It happened because he was so high he thought he would be able to swim across."

I sit there still, looking at her. There's something that's typical in what she's said of the pattern of our marriage, her insistence on oversimplifying and her inability to grasp my motives.

"You tried to make it Kay's fault, like one person could pay and then we could keep going," she says when I don't respond. She picks up the stack of books on the desk and sets them in the box, closing it up. "I'm glad Kay didn't get convicted."

"You've chosen your friendship with Ellen over everything else," I tell her, trying to get at the bottom layer. "That's why you're arguing about moral integrity now. That's why you're picking at the smaller points. Kay didn't even get convicted."

She turns away from me, picking up the black hat and smoothing the top of it with her hand. "I'm not going with you," she says.

"What do you mean?" I lean back against the monkey, aware suddenly of how tired I am, washed away.

"I'm not moving. I took a job with Sandy. It's part-time, but the veterinary assistant she has is leaving in November, and then she can give me more hours. I'm going to rent a place near Deerfield."

She turns the hat over in her hands, staring into it. I'm remembering that it has an absurd pouch at the top that opens up to reveal a concealed stuffed rabbit. Cards came with it, and a set of handcuffs.

"I don't want to leave the support groups I'm in right now, and I need some time to try to work out what's happened." She looks up at me, and there's a slight tremble in her lips, the hardness that was there moments ago replaced by uncertainty.

"They'll have support groups in upstate New York," I assure her. "You could find one there."

She looks back down at the hat. "Sandy knows of a house I can rent. I went over there this morning, actually, and signed a one-year lease."

I close my eyes. The monkey behind me is soft and full of lumps. There's part of me that can't imagine ever getting off the bed. "It's because of Ellen, isn't it?" I ask finally.

"No, it's not that." She pauses for a moment, and when I open my eyes, she's looking at me almost as if something in her regrets what she's said. "Ellen doesn't even know I'm staying."

We sit there for moment, as she turns the hat over again and runs her hands around the rim. Then she sets it back on the desk. "I'm sorry," she says, glancing at me before she leaves the room and goes downstairs. A few minutes later I hear the car start up in the driveway.

I lie there for a while thinking about what she's said. It's apparent to me suddenly that the moral imperative she follows is stronger than my own—simpler, and less capable of embracing the complications of what's happened, but purer. It is what I loved about her even before we were married. I picture her the way she was then, clear and exacting. When I was hot with emotion, she was like drinking a glass of cool water.

My body feels leaden. I get up slowly from the bed and walk over to the desk. The hat lies on it upside down, and I put my hand inside, feeling for the stuffed rabbit, but the pouch is empty. Sometimes at night David and Michael would put on magic shows for Jen and me after dinner. The routines they made up were so funny we would laugh until we cried. Then Jen would heat cocoa on the stove or scoop ice cream into bowls and cover it with a layer of chocolate syrup.

I set down the hat and open the box and take the book from it that Jen was reading. Inside it are tiny drawings—coiled snakes, boats, planes, faces, various animals, and abstract designs done in ink. A cryptic detail, as if, for some reason I'll never get, he drew his way through the literature of his childhood.

It's dark now almost everywhere, except for the piece of light on the desk. I think I hear Jen's car returning, but when I look out the window, the driveway's empty. Maybe it is our failure to understand one another that lies at the heart of everything.

I get up and stand by the doorway. There's a trick of light in the corner where a blanket's been thrown on top of some cushions, and it looks as if a child could be sleeping there. Now when I try to picture the way he was at nineteen, the year before his death, I can't. You do everything you can think of, but nothing brings him back, and that nothing wells up until it consumes you.

Michael

THAT AFTERNOON WHEN they took the acid, David tried to talk me into it. "You won't get addicted," he said. "It's not even that strong. One is like a half dose."

They had driven back from school together earlier that day. I was practicing my shots on the driveway, already feeling like a third wheel.

"It'll make you see things differently," he told me as I punched the basketball through the net. "Where the ball ends up won't matter."

"But I want it to matter."

"The hoop will turn into the ring of God."

"Or the ring of an ass."

I walked to the river with them, and they swallowed it down with a bottle of Coke. Mom was roasting a chicken and baking potatoes, clueless. David made jokes about how they'd be sitting around at supper stoned.

"Pass the potatoes. Let me have some of that salad. Let me eat the forest," he said, and Kay laughed so hard the Coke came out of her nose.

Much later that night, when we were out driving, just before we stopped on the bridge, I tried to get David to drive up a different road. "Pull over," I said, slamming my knee against the back of the front seat. "Go up the fire road."

Fire roads, built for the trucks owned by the rangers, run up the mountains to the towers. The last time I'd been up one was at the end of the summer, when Kay and I had sat at the top talking for hours.

"We'd get stuck," David told me. "It's been too wet."

"I'd rather get stuck on a fire road than sit on the train tracks." Over the edge of the seat I could see their hands on each other's jeans, like they could screw each other on the front seat and I wouldn't know.

By the time we stopped on the bridge, I hated them both. They were talking to each other and calling out something to me, but anything that was said got swallowed by the sound of the river.

When they wouldn't come back, I got in the car and tried to fit the key David had left on the seat into the ignition. There was a long time when they were making out, and I wanted to grind them under the tires. Then David got up on the rail and raised his arms over his head. In the distance I could make out the roundness of the hills. I could see the outline of the trees on the shore. It took a long time. Kay had her hands on his pants, as if they were making a kind of love. And then he was gone.

I let him jump because I'm in love with her, I thought immediately.

After that, everything else happened all at once—Kay's foot raised as she tried to climb onto the rail and the way she fell when I pulled her away and fought to drag her back to the car, hitting her in the face.

By the time the hearings took place, all that lay buried. The last time I saw her was in the courtroom. I had been meeting with a grief counselor at school. Denial is the first stage, then anger, sadness, and loss. The problem is, I keep circling back, so the stages are mixed up, and I feel like I could be doing them forever.

"It was my fault," I told the counselor.

"You were in the car when he fell," he answered me. "You didn't push him."

"I didn't even yell out to him to stop. Then I tore up the bridge when I saw that she was going to jump also. She had one foot on the rail when I pulled her away."

"You saved her life, then. You can't blame yourself for not being able to save him also."

In the courtroom the prosecutor asked Kay why she hadn't jumped. "You had helped him to jump, and then you stepped away?"

"Yes," she answered.

She doesn't remember. It's been seven years now. I'm living alone after graduating from college, and sometimes, while I'm cooking or eating a meal, I talk out loud, as if David and Kay are in the room and can hear me.

"Hey," David calls out. "They got this drowning stuff wrong. Existence is in the mind."

There's a girl I was dating for a while, someone who asked me out my last year of college, even though I was shut tight as a drum. "It's not a crime that you loved her," she said one night after I'd been talking about David's death again. "It doesn't make you guilty. He was so messed up. How could you be expected to understand what went on between them?"

I tried to explain it, how there is too much guilt, how I am completely screwed up.

"You're still in love with her," she said before she broke up with me. "No one else can measure up."

The counselor thought I needed to separate myself from what Kay and David chose to do when they were standing at the edge of the bridge looking over the rail. "It was a kind of craziness," he told me. "David wanted to jump, not because he sensed that you loved Kay, maybe not even because he wanted the two of them united, but for his own disturbed reasons. A drug can do that. It can make anyone delusional."

"The guilt will get you nowhere." Another thing he told me after I said that I had pummeled Kay while trying to get her off the bridge. "The trial's over. She wasn't convicted."

A year ago my father remarried, and he's living a second life now near Albany. Becca is in her thirties, and recently he said they were hoping for a baby. For a while after the trial he talked about pursuing a civil case against Kay. Once when he was visiting me, I tried to talk to him about David. "It's like you never even knew him. Just because he was brilliant, you thought he was perfect. He was the one to take all the risks, not Kay. He was always like that."

But my father always had a way of putting you on the defensive. "Are you still that jealous of him?" he asked me.

I was a junior then, and if both he and Mom came to watch my game, they would sit apart, like they didn't know one another. I think that at first after he moved away, he tried to talk her into coming with him, but she had already found a house by then, a small one built around the turn of the century in the town of Deerfield, just a few houses down from the veterinarian's where she was working.

I visit with her regularly, staying for the weekend every month or two. She still does animal-rescue work for the wildlife organization and spends long hours working with Sandy. Twice a week she volunteers at the elementary school. I don't think she's dated since my father left, but her phone is constantly ringing with people who've found an animal that needs help or who have a problem with a pet.

Sometimes while I'm there, I drive by the old house. It looks the same. The people who moved in didn't even change the curtains. Once I saw Ellen in her yard and stopped to talk with her and ended up writing down Kay's address and phone number.

I graduated a year ago, and just recently I accepted a job working for the forestry department in Maine doing wildlife preservation and conservation planning. I'll live in one of their trailers and drive to the towers, where I'll scan the trees looking for fires.

"Drive up the fire road." It all comes rushing back.

In March the water beneath the bridge is more than thirty feet deep, stirred up by the current, full of silt and leaf matter. It's impossible to see down there, even with the lights that divers use. At the bottom, where it's darkest, there are embedded fossils. Downstream, where an old railroad bridge is submerged, the wooden ties sometimes float to the surface, and you can find an iron spike driven into the bank.

David and I were opposites—the fearless and the cowardly, the brilliant and the dull. My father still has large folders he filled with any information or articles he could find about the river, as if by sheer volume they would explain something.

I've been rehearsing what I would say if Kay agrees to see me when I drive through Boston. Her mother told me she lives alone there and works in one of the hospitals. "You know," she said, standing on the roadside next to all those flowers, "I don't think she's ever gotten over it."

Sometimes I still wonder how life is on the other side. Did he watch the search the next day? Did he sit in the courtroom?

When the river level is up, it covers the tree trunks so that the budding limbs spread out above the surface. In my dreams I see it like that—the straight span of pavement with the steel arch underneath, the low railing, the rough, dark water and the sunken trees. Often I am buried in it, moving slowly through the cold current, past the waving, waterlogged limbs and the weeds that have died back during the winter. Sometimes there is a shoe, a dark sneaker embedded. Sometimes a hand, a piece of denim.

"David . . ." I wake up with the sound of the bullhorn in my head or in a cold sweat, unable to get my breath. It was cold that night, and damp, as if the air had picked up pieces of the river. He went to the edge, then climbed onto the rail while I watched from the car. "I didn't even open the car door," I told the counselor.

"You were horrified," he answered. "People often can't react immediately when they see something like that."

What David didn't know is that the rest of us would have to keep going. For a long time it pissed me off. Once I drove out there and stood where he stood. "You son of a bitch!" I yelled over the edge. "You fucking son of a bitch!"

Now I have a range of feelings—resentment, loss, anger, love, guilt—the gamut. "That's a sign that you're healed," the counselor said, as if the game could be finished.

"So you're telling me I'm stuck with all this the rest of my life."

"That's being alive, Michael. We're all stuck with what happens to us."

In the end there's no resolution. You just have to resolve yourself to it. So I'll head up to Maine and look for fires. Maybe Kay will talk to me, and the past will unravel.

The water was close to freezing that night. I went back to the car, pissed off, and sat in it watching. Just get this over with so I can go the hell home, I remember thinking. There was a big game scheduled a couple of nights later and a practice I needed to go to the next morning. He stood up on the rail, and then I saw his body fall toward the river.

"David!" I yelled. "You fuck, David!"

He was already underwater by then. There was the sound of his body as it hit the surface and then nothing. Just the echoes, the reverberations that last a lifetime.

Kay

IT'S JUNE, A midsummer afternoon, and we run through the pasture across the road, where the grass is filled with Queen Anne's lace, blue chicory, and black-eyed Susans, a collage of grass, flowers, and sky.

"I'm going to make this stay, everything just as it is," he says, and the sound of his voice hangs in the air, shining and clear. I reach out. I pull him toward me.

"I love you," I tell him, and he says it back, the words bright as silver. We say it over and over, until everything is one sound, singing across the field.

Pale blue, white lace—even when I shut my eyes, the flowers seem to move, dappled across my eyelids. We lie down among them for so long it is as if we're drunk on the light. The air is shimmering and still, layered with the flowers and the winged insects and butterflies, the high-pitched hum of brightness. It is forever that I am there, David's body over mine, his fingers smoothing my face, his mouth on my mouth, our skin dissolving until we are all field and singing.

It's only when we sit up and put on our clothing, that I see how fragile it is, how the light hangs thick and unmoving, as if everything is about to disappear. We stand, ready to walk through the field, and the image is drawn out, David's body stretched skyward, arms extended, falling through the air.

I TRY TO put it together again, then go back and pick it apart. I loved him because he was smart and funny and unafraid, because he made me unafraid. And maybe he loved who I was, or maybe he loved who I was when he was with me, the way I changed when he was there.

I try to touch the intensity. Sometimes I think it was because we'd known each other since childhood. I knew from inside the way his body moved. I could taste what he ate, I could see what he saw. A bond that erased the fact of singularity.

Maybe it is beyond explanation. I would be who he wanted, bigger and more than myself. I would jump off the bridge, I would swim hard across the river.

One morning, after the trial, Jen came over to the barn to talk with my mother. "I'm sorry," she said. "I didn't want this, but I couldn't talk about it while it was going on, not with anyone." My mother kept sculpting. She told me later she hadn't looked up. "I'm divorcing Kevin," Jen told her as she left.

Maybe all of us spin our lives out in nonsensical patterns. A few months later, when Jen was moving to Deerfield, my mother walked over to say good-bye to her. Kevin had already left by then, and much of the house was empty. "I want you to take this," my mother said and handed her a mask she had made several years earlier using Jen's face as a model. The mask had Jen's features—the long nose, rounded cheekbones, and pointed chin, but the forehead peeled away, and there was something mysterious and transforming in the openness of the curves.

Jen took it from her and laid it on the kitchen table. It was one of my mother's best pieces, something she had shown in a gallery in New York City and had refused to sell even though there had been a substantial offer.

"Thank you," she said. Then for a long minute she looked directly at my mother, and my mother said later she knew then that they probably wouldn't talk with one another again.

"You were a good friend," Jen told her as she was leaving. And my mother nodded yes before she walked out of their house.

When I try to understand David or rebuild who he was, I end up with a kind of shell and a mixture of contradictory impressions. Then, when I'm not thinking about him, there he is suddenly, as if he could be standing next to me.

Maybe my mother and I, out of our own aloneness, would have bonded with whoever was living in that house next to ours. If there was a woman, my mother would have befriended her. If there was a boy, I would have fallen in love with him.

When I watch my friends and the young people I work with pairing off like partners in a dance, I think we fill each other, we connect because we have to. But I'd like to think that sometimes we touch what is true or genuine in the other person, that mysteriousness in each of us that makes us both recognizable and intangible.

I've quit my job at the hospital, moved out of my apartment, and driven back home to leave some of my things with my mother—Kee-Kee and her wooden cage, the table I painted blue, a poster from my wall, my collection of crimson plates. My mother worries that I've left a good job with no sense of where I'll go. She's asked me to move in with her for a while, to "stay grounded," while I consider my options.

But I'm taking the money from my savings account and going far away to Europe first, then maybe to Africa or China. When I was in college, I thought about getting a degree in botany. Maybe when I'm done traveling, I'll find a job working in a plant conservatory or a nursery.

Last month Michael came to visit me. We went out to a coffee shop to talk, then found a place to have dinner. He spent the night sleeping on the couch in my apartment.

"I pulled you away from the rail that night," he told me. "After David jumped, I ran up the walkway, and you had one foot on the rail, as if you were climbing onto it. The mark they found was from your shoe."

I could see the scuff mark, dirt on the black paint.

"You started fighting me, and I swung at you. I hit you in the face." He was crying by then. "I thought you were crazy. I thought you both were."

"I would have jumped?"

We had eaten dinner by then and were walking back to my apartment. I stopped on the busy sidewalk, and he turned to look at me.

"I told my father when the trial was over. He said it wouldn't have made a difference, and all it meant was that I had saved you.

He said David wouldn't have jumped off the rail, and the focus of everything was you pushing him."

He looked at me strangely for a minute, as if he didn't recognize me—my thin face, I thought, the close-cropped hair. "I should have said it at the trial."

I nodded slightly, not wanting to think about the trial. Then, after another minute, we started walking again. The stores along the sidewalk were lit up and full of people coming and going. "My father didn't know David," Michael said. "David wasn't afraid of anything. When we were kids, he would always swing out higher than you or me on that rope over the river, and the way he used to dive from the rocks even though everyone told us not to. My father saw him as perfect. He would have gone on to be some kind of scholar. I was lucky to make it through college."

I took his arm for a minute as we crossed the street. "It was hard to get through anything after that night. I never went back to college."

"You know, my father came to visit me one afternoon, and he took me out to dinner. I was a junior, and he'd gotten my latest set of grades in the mail. 'You can do better than this,' he said, and he took the paper out of his pocket and laid it on the table between our plates.

" 'Not without a transplant,' I told him.

" 'Be glad that you're alive,' he says. 'You, at least, have the chance to excel.' Then he told me he'd decided I had to quit basketball. He would pay the full tuition my senior year. After that, my grades got worse. He never understood either one of us."

I would have jumped. Somehow that's easier to live with.

are cut flowers on the table—cosmos, foxgloves, and roses. A painting of water, a yellow boat. In her small wooden house at the edge of a cornfield by the river.

A separateness I have inherited like a genetic mutation, the closet skeleton. The rooms look different from year to year. She moves the furniture around even if no one else sits in it. She changes the pots and pans.

"I could have gotten an abortion," she said one night when we were up late talking. "That's what he asked me to do, but I wanted you. Oh, I wanted you, even though I knew he was leaving for California. 'I've always wanted to see it,' he said. 'I get restless. I can't come home to the same place every night. I hate repetition.' "

My father was gone, but David and Michael and their parents took his place. For fifteen years they filled us up. "Come down to the river, Kay. Run through the field, Kay."

The animals Jen healed. The pieces of clay my mother laid out in the sun, taken hot from the kiln. The flock of students. David and Michael running through the rows of corn or swinging out on a branch over the river.

They invited us sometimes for holidays and for weekend nights out onto the lawn, smoking ears of corn on the fire, sparklers spun on the dark drive.

This afternoon, when I drove up to their house, I noticed it was for sale again. The people who had bought it from Jen and Kevin had already moved out, and it was empty.

"It looks deserted," I tell my mother as I sit down to eat the dinner she's made for us. "The grass is grown high, and the lights are all off."

"Why would you have done it?" he asked when we were back at my apartment getting out the extra sheets to make a bed up for him on the couch.

"I don't know. Maybe because nothing else mattered, because being with him mattered so much."

We talked for a long time that night about how maybe that was love, wanting so much to be with someone that you don't think about anything else, you don't think. Or maybe it was being high. And we talked about the risk-taking and the drive for perfection and how they were part of the same thing. The more David became perfect, the more dangerous were the risks he had to take.

"You're still romanticizing it," Michael said. "It was self-destructive."

We didn't talk about what had happened after the memorial service by the river, but the next morning when he was leaving, he said, "You know, I was jealous of David, because I'd always loved you also."

A week later, when I decided to quit my job and go overseas, I called to tell him. He asked me to write when I got there and said that if I stayed, he would come and visit me.

When I told my mother I'd seen Michael, she seemed happy that we had talked. She said she hoped it would help us find some peace. As I've gotten older, I've grown closer to her. She's good at being alone, singing in her kitchen where no one can hear her, laughing. She keeps bowls she's made arranged on the counter—one for fruit, one filled with nuts, another with squash or ripening tomatoes. Some of her masks and sculptures sit on the shelves or in the corners of her rooms. In the summer there

"Nothing," I said. "She admitted that she pushed him, and they didn't even find her guilty."

There was a pause while we drove past the reporters and news cameras. "You dragged us all through this for nothing," she told me.

I find her now in David's room, bent over the pile of things on his desk. There's a partially deflated football, a stack of books, and a black hat.

"What are you doing?" I ask, standing in the doorway, one hand against the jamb.

The answer seems obvious enough that she doesn't say it. For several minutes I stand there, watching her. One of the books is open on the desk, and she seems to be reading it.

"You could leave this for the moving company," I tell her. "I was going to call them and see if they could get us up there this month instead of next. The house that the college is letting us use is already available."

I sit down on David's bed. It has a blue spread with a comforter folded at the bottom and a pillow we bought for him years ago in the shape of a monkey.

"Ellen called earlier today," she says, looking up from the book. "She's staying at her mother's out at the Cape."

"You spoke to her?"

She pauses for a minute, closing the book. "She wanted to know why our house was on the market, and I told her you'd taken the job in upstate New York. She said she didn't understand anything that had happened. She said it was like a nightmare. I said yes, it still is."

"What did she say to that?"

"She said that nothing can ever be the same again."

"Does she think it's our fault, like if we hadn't asked for the police investigation, Kay would be finishing a second year of college and we'd all be friends?"

"No. She was just saying that we had been friends for almost fifteen years and then we were suddenly enemies because of one night and something that happened when neither one of us was there. She was saying how strange that was."

She sits there for a moment, looking at me, and I see that she's older than she looked a year ago, with new lines on her face and a worn expression. "What did you finally do with the drugs you found in his dorm room?"

We sit there for a moment without my answering. Most of the time when we've talked during the last several months, I've felt like she wasn't listening. Whenever I've tried to explain myself, she's busied herself taking care of the cat she adopted or talking at the same time to Michael or answering the phone.

"Did you flush them down the toilet before they searched the house?" she asks, putting down the book she was holding and turning to face me. "Did you bury them?"

"If I had handed them over, it wouldn't have changed anything," I answer slowly.

She shakes her head, listening but not hearing anything. "You're outraged because his death is being recorded as accidental or as a possible suicide, when you're certain it wasn't. Yet you destroyed evidence so that it would look like Kay might have supplied the drugs that night."

"She could have," I say evenly. "There's no way to know if

There are plates glazed with bright colors set out on the table in the kitchen, pasta covered with a red sauce, the dark green leaves of a salad. In her bathroom I've seen a box with iodine, bandages, and a rubber dropper in it. Sometimes she takes in an injured cat or squirrel or rabbit. There's a cage she keeps out back, to abate the carnage, to keep back the flood.

"I don't go over there anymore," she says. "I never got to know the couple who bought it." For a while she thought about moving into a house or an apartment closer to the university. She even spent one spring looking with a real-estate agent. But in the end she couldn't give up her workshop or her flowers.

Recently she had a showing of her clay masks at a gallery in New York City, and there's another one scheduled for next spring. Each semester she teaches two courses, and she goes out regularly to the movies.

"Jen doesn't contact me, even though we live close by," she says. "I hear about her sometimes through a friend. Her phone number's listed. I've thought about calling, but I don't know what I would say."

I've rehearsed different versions of what I would say to Jen. "I loved him." Or "I'm sorry."

We finish eating supper, and I tell my mother I want to walk down and see the house. Initially she says she'll clean up the kitchen while I go over and that afterward we'll drive into town for dessert or a movie, but as I'm leaving, she stops me.

"I'll go with you," she calls as she follows me out into the yard. "I'd like to see the place again. I haven't been over there in years."

Jen and my mother's gardens have spread out to cover more and more of the yards. I can see them from the road—the pink and white phlox, the blue cornflowers and purple irises, the lace hydrangea and the roses. Sometimes cars pull over for several minutes to drink it up.

I close my eyes for a moment and listen. It is still early in the evening, and the sun is warm and yellow. There are birds in the trees, and in the fields I can hear the high hum of insects. Already I can feel inside myself the paths I could take to get there.

"It's been empty for three months now," my mother says as we reach the edge of the yard. "I heard there's an investor who's interested in buying it and renting it out to students. This far from the college, I can't imagine who he'd get."

The curtains Jen made are still on the windows in the front of the house, and a clay pot my mother made years ago sits on the stoop. We walk around to the side. In places the white paint is chipping, and there's a drain spout that's fallen and is lying on the ground. "Nothing's been done to keep this place up," my mother says.

We go to the kitchen window, which is curtainless, and peer through it into the house. The counters and cabinets look the same, and the refrigerator and stove haven't been changed. I remember a set of plates my mother made for Jen one year, and the large kettle that sat on the stove on winter afternoons. There was a wooden table against one of the walls and six chairs.

"Remember the parties they had here?" my mother asks. "Once, when it was my birthday, friends of ours from the university came over. I can remember the chocolate cake Jen helped you decorate with flowers you cut from our garden. We went outside in the dark and had music playing. We danced on the grass, and Jen taught David and you and Michael dances like the tango. She had you dance with one and then the other."

We walk out across the back of the yard, and I can remember being held by them around the waist, leaping to the music. The sweatiness of their hands, the smell of their bodies mixing with the smells of a summer night and the corn we'd roasted earlier and the river.

"It seemed like you would end up marrying one of them. I used to worry over which one it would be. Jen always thought it would be Michael."

We go out to the shed where Jen kept her animals. It's been turned into a little garage now, with a door that is easy to open, and we swing it out and walk inside. It's smaller than I remember, and it's hard to picture the table Jen had in the corner, the cages and the box of supplies. There are shelves still lining one wall, and somehow, when I close my eyes, I smell the earthy, animal scent.

We walk outside again into the yard, and for a moment I can hear their voices, David's and Michael's, calling out. I can hear their laughter. *I'm still here,* I want to say. But a wind blows up through the limbs of a large oak overhead, and my mother says we should start back if we want to drive into town.

After David died, I read the copy of *Hamlet* that Jen gave me with his notes written in the margins. "David understood love," I tell my mother, still trying to justify something. "And everything he did was full of meaning. He always had a plan, even when we were younger, like when we dug out caves by the river or when we made those forts or ran through the fields."

"When you took the acid," she interjects. "When he decided you should jump off the bridge.

"I see him differently is all," she adds. For years now she's counseled me on her version of things: David as leader, me as follower. He wanted to fly everywhere and see the world, and he ended up seeing none of it.

I have enough money saved to travel for several months and find myself somewhere else. I've booked a flight to Greece, where Sara, who has remained my one close friend, teaches English. She's said I can stay with her as long as I want. She's been writing to me for a year now about the apartment she has next to the sea. She spends her weekends exploring the nearby islands in a small motorboat. There are fresh fish and olives, goat cheese and fruit.

As my mother and I walk across the yard and out onto the road, I see it again in my head, the hard curve of the metal bar under my feet and palms, the shakiness of my balance, the moment when I let go and straighten, stretching into the air. Then the movement outward, the tightening and release of my thighs, the enormous speed of the fall.

As always, he is there. If not in the cold, dark water where we struggle to pull one another to shore, then on the other side, a spill of light, a silken brilliance.

Bright net. Feather. White bone. As if he is folded inside, a shadow.

There was a long time when I was quiet, after the trial, when I didn't say anything, when I didn't seem to hear, only what I had to. I got up in the morning and went to work at Sara's mother's store. I came home in the afternoon and made dinner.

One thing after another, next and next, like river water settling in summer, once the current has died and the level has fallen.

He didn't think. He raised his arms and jumped from the railing, but I haven't been able to give it up—the bird flying from her cage, talking late at night, a good cup of coffee. He is down deep, deep down in me.

"Too much water hast thou . . ."

With his dark hair, in one piece, wearing his skin. Not full of water or his bones burned, feather white. Skin touching skin, our mouths, the triangle of hair between our legs. One second spreading out. The way my hands move through his hair, chest to chest, thigh to thigh.

I'll fly to Greece, where the sun is like honey. The turquoise water and island flowers. As if I could wash him away. As if I could fly him.

Beyond the river, like a shadow stitched to the soul.

"No, no, he is dead; Go to thy deathbed; He never will come again."

I didn't have a father, but I had two brothers.

One, a year older, one a year younger. And we would run through the fields to the river.